ONE HUNDRED MISTAKES

AN ASPEN COVE SMALL TOWN ROMANCE

KELLY COLLINS

BOOK NOOK PRESS

CHAPTER ONE

Deanna Archer rushed from the Corner Store with sweat on her brow and a tingle on her lips. Why in the hell did she kiss Merrick? Sure, he was handsome and single, but holy hell, what compelled her to fist his shirt and pull him down for a lip-locking kiss? He was the new deputy sheriff and could have arrested her for sexual harassment, but instead, he agreed to have pizza and beer with her at six.

She stopped at the curb and took several cleansing breaths, but her heart whirled faster, like a cyclone out of control.

"What the hell was that about?" Red said from behind her.

She steeled her shoulders. "That was about self-preservation. My mom once told me you could lead a horse to water, but you can't make him drink. You're the horse, Red, and I'm the water, but my well is running dry. No, scratch that, you're a donkey, and I've had enough of you being an ass."

"So, you kiss Merrick?"

She brought her fingers to her lips and felt the heat the sheriff left behind. "I guess I did."

"You're not having dinner with him, are you?" He stood with his legs spread and chest pushed out like he was showing off a coat of armor.

She glanced at her phone to see the time. "I don't have time to waste discussing my love life when I have to prepare for my date." She pivoted and started for home.

"I know what you're doing," he yelled after her. "You're trying to make me jealous, but it won't work because I'm not the jealous type."

She lifted her hand in the air and waved like she didn't have a care in the world, when in reality, she had at least a dozen starting with, what in the hell was she thinking? She had a date with Merrick. Was it a date? Surely, he knew it wasn't a *date* date. He was in law enforcement and most likely could read a bluff.

Her fingers felt her lips again. *It sure felt real, though.*

But it wasn't, because as much as she wanted someone to choose her, love her, and be her prince charming, those stories only happened on the Hall-mark Channel, romance novels, and The Bachelor. There was no one waiting to gift her with a rose.

She considered her "date." With only a take-and-bake pizza from Dalton's shop and a six-pack of beer to offer, she was woefully unprepared. At the corner, she crossed the street and backtracked to the bakery. If Merrick showed up, she'd let him know it was an impulsive act, a gut reaction to Red being an idiot. If he was cool with her rationale, there was no reason they couldn't have dinner and a beer to-gether. She'd pick up some of Katie's sweets to make his evening less of a waste.

Red stood across the street, scowling at her. "Forgot dessert," she called over to him. It probably wasn't smart to poke a bear, but he deserved her wrath. They had sex, and after that, he ghosted her. Now she had to see him every single day at work and wonder why in the hell she didn't measure up.

As she neared B's Bakery, the rich aroma of dark chocolate wrapped around her and tugged her into the shop where Katie sat across from Sage under The Wishing Wall. Though Sage wasn't due to have her baby until November, she looked ready to pop.

"Deanna," Katie squealed. She always was up-beat and happy. Maybe working with sweets in-stead of assholes was the key. "Do you have time for coffee?" She hopped up and grabbed another chair from a nearby wrought iron table, pulling it to theirs. "I just made a batch of caramel pecan brownies. It's a new recipe, and you can be the guinea pig."

She glanced at the wall clock and shrugged. "I've got a few minutes." She plunked into the seat and looked at The Wishing Wall, and then her eyes went to Sage. "What's it like making a human?"

"Exhausting. Who knew it would be so hard? I mean, women have been doing it since the beginning of time. One would think it was easy. If men had to pay to have their wives make a baby, they couldn't afford it. If they had to have the babies, civilization would have ended thousands of years ago."

A ripple moved across Sage's belly. "Did the baby just move?"

"He never stays still."

Deanna sat up. "It's a he?"

Sage laughed. "It's a he when it's a beast and a she when all is calm." She reached over and grabbed Deanna's hand, pulling her forward and setting her palm on the top of her stomach. Seconds later, a wave of movement happened. "We don't know the sex. There are very few surprises in life, and this will be one of them."

Katie returned with a cup of coffee and a brownie oozing caramel. "Tell me what you think.

Don't hold back. It's a turtle brownie. I know it's not anything groundbreaking because other bakeries make them, but this is my first try." She took her seat and waited for Deanna to take a bite.

She pulled the warm confection to her lips, the same lips Merrick kissed. When she tasted it, she knew she'd been transported from her temporary hell to sweet heaven.

"Oh. My. God, I'll take a half dozen of these. I've got a date with Merrick and came here for dessert, so these are perfect."

Both women cocked their heads.

"Mountain of a man, Merrick? Deputy Sheriff Merrick, who is as sweet as those brownies?" Katie asked.

With a roll of her eyes, Deanna swallowed and attempted to explain. She gave them the short and dirty version that went from her one-night stand with Red to her unexplainable date tonight with Merrick.

"He had drunk sex with you and then ghosted you?" Sage asked.

"I wouldn't call it drunk sex. I was in the studio one night while he was putting down some tracks. He had a bottle of wine and offered me a glass." The next part was embarrassing. "I can drink a Russian under the table if we're downing vodka, but give me one glass of wine, and I'm done."

"It's the tannins," Sage said. "I know lots of people who can drink hard liquor but give them a little fermented grape juice, and they're dancing on the tables."

Deanna hung her head. "Or screwing on the hood of his car." She let out a groan. "Worst decision ever."

"That bad, huh?" Katie reached over and picked a piece of brownie off Deanna's plate.

"No, it was good. I didn't see stars or anything, but that was because the ridge of the hood was digging into my back."

"You were actually on the hood?" Sage closed her eyes as if she were trying to imagine it. "Wouldn't he have to be Merrick tall for that to work?"

She was right. Merrick was tall. Deanna had to drag him down to kiss him.

"It was more of an against the car scenario, and maybe it was the front grill that was so uncomfortable."

"The man has no class." Katie stretched her lips into a thin line. "First time, and it was against a car? You don't need him. He's not a keeper." She tapped her finger on her lips. "He's a catch and release."

"You don't understand. I really like him. I've known him for a long time." Why she felt the need to defend Red, she didn't know. Was she defending him or herself for making poor choices? If he wasn't so bad, then that meant her decision-making skills weren't awful either. Why did she feel the need to lie to herself? Right now, Red was the worst of the worst, but she still liked him. There was no accounting for taste.

Sage got up and walked around the counter to grab an oat bran muffin. They were another staple in the bakery's daily offerings. She held it up. "A girl needs her bran. Did you know that pregnancy totally messes up your digestive system?" She took a bite and talked around it. "I knew it, but I didn't think it would happen to me." She took her seat. "Let's get back to Red. Is he really the guy you want?"

She considered the question because they had a history, and she knew him better than any man. Knew his quirks, like how he played the opening riff to *Another One Bites the Dust* before each session. He preferred blueberry muffins to cranberry orange and liked cheap red wine, which was why she got a headache, or maybe it was because she was so frustrated with him on the regular that he'd given her an aneurysm.

He didn't know she heard him tell the band they were a mistake because she'd marched out of the studio after lobbing a muffin at his head. But the sound guy had the room on speaker, and she took in every hurtful word when he said they had too much wine and made several poor choices.

Since then, she mostly kept her distance, but she noticed him looking at her. She knew the flowers on her doorstep last week were from him. There weren't many single men in Aspen Cove. There was Gray, the guitarist, but he was more like a brother. Then there was Merrick, who probably didn't know she existed until she accosted him. The flowers were from Red, but why had he dropped them off? Were they a sign of attraction or an apology? She hadn't considered the motive, only that they arrived.

"I want Red. Better the devil you know, right?"

Both Katie and Sage frowned, but only Katie spoke. "The best way to get a man is to pretend you don't want him. Rejection is a hard pill to swallow."

Sage finished her last bite of bran muffin. "You deserve better than what he's giving you. If you want him, make him work for it. Merrick is the perfect decoy. Just make sure he knows where he stands. It would be awful to lead him on when you don't have any intention of pursuing a relationship." She stood. "Kind of sounds like what Red did to you." She covered her mouth and gasped. "Oh, did I say that out loud?" She moved toward the door. "I swear I have no filter anymore. It must be the hormones."

Katie laughed so hard, she snorted. "You never had a filter. You want an honest answer?" She pointed at Sage. "That girl has it."

"I'm out of here. I think the bran is working." Sage walked out the door, leaving Katie and Deanna alone.

"Do you think I'm being silly?"

Katie waved her hand through the air. "Girl, I fell in love with Bowie. He didn't know he wanted me until I convinced him of the truth, and that was he couldn't live without me. Love wants what love wants."

Deanna looked up and pointed to The Wishing Wall. "What are the chances it works?"

Katie grabbed a pen and a yellow sticky note from the board. "It can't work if you don't try." She placed them on the table in front of Deanna.

"There's been so much change in my life lately, and I just want a constant. I want to be loved by someone besides my poodle, Sherman."

"Sherman?"

"Don't laugh, but while I was hugging him in the pet store, deciding if he was the one, I swear he said, 'My name is Sherman.' Who was I to argue?" She plopped the last bite into her mouth, and after she savored and swallowed, she continued. "No one was more surprised than me to walk out with a poodle named Sherman. I didn't even like that breed. I went in to get a Yorkie."

Katie rose and walked behind the display case. "I've found that sometimes we don't get a choice in who we end up with. You'd think you do, but if it's not right, it won't ever work." She packed six beautiful gooey brownies and placed the box on the counter. "My contribution to your journey to love." She pointed to the sticky note. "Put your wish on the board. You never know who's watching or listening. Maybe you have a guardian angel, or the universe wants to shine on you."

Deanna picked up the box and tucked a twenty into the tip jar. She knew the money never went to the staff. It was donated to whoever needed something, and that was fine by her. When she turned to leave, she stopped and wrote on the sticky note before pinning it to the wall. There had to be at least a dozen wishes already in place. It felt silly wishing for something as fundamental as love, but a person always wanted what they didn't have.

Right now, she had a half dozen brownies and a fake date with Merrick Buchanan. Could her life get any more complicated?

CHAPTER TWO

Merrick walked out baffled. He'd gone to the Corner Store for a frozen meal and walked out with a date. How did that happen?

Outside, Red stood staring at the bakery. Just inside the window, Merrick could see Deanna.

"Hey man, if she's your girl, I can call off the pizza and beer."

Red swung around to face him. His muscles tensed, and his eyes narrowed to slits. "She's not mine. Do what you want, but let me warn you," he glanced over his shoulder at the bakery. "That girl is clingy. If you kiss her, she'll want a ring and house with a white picket fence."

Merrick laughed. "Then I better get shopping for that ring and putting up that fence."

Red's eyes grew large. "I'm serious, man. That one,"—he thumbed behind him—"she's a forever girl. If you just want a taste, then I'd say dine somewhere else."

A little tornado of agitation spun in Merrick's gut. He was raised by a single mother and had a little sister, so he was sensitive to women's feelings, and no woman he knew would have found Red's words flattering. Maybe the part about *forever girl* if used in a different context, like she was the kind of girl a man would want to keep forever, but that's not what Red meant. He got his taste and moved on to another appetizer.

"You're an asshole."

Red shrugged. "I've been called worse."

"I can see why."

Red scowled. "Aren't you supposed to be here to serve and protect? What part of your job does busting my balls fall into?"

Merrick straightened to his full six-foot-four-inch frame and stared down at Red. Most men would cower, but Red stood defiant.

"That would be the part described as serve and protect. Something you might not understand because I'm pretty sure the words respect and honor aren't part of your vernacular."

"My what?"

Merrick shook his head. "Look it up. It starts

with a *V* in case you were confused." That small tornado was growing in size and strength. He was generally an easygoing guy, but he didn't have much tolerance for people who mistreated women or animals. "Do you want me to spell it out for you?"

"Now who's being the asshole?" Red asked.

Merrick turned back toward the store. "I've been called worse." He walked inside and straight to the cooler to grab a bottle of water.

"You okay?" The woman behind the counter asked. He hadn't met her yet because she was a new transplant.

"Yep, just need a cool down." He twisted the lid from the bottle and gulped.

"Hot from the kiss?"

He stretched his neck from right to left until several vertebrae clicked into place. "It started there but ended with a pain in my ass."

Her perfectly plucked brows lifted. "I'd say your neck by the way you're popping it. Turn around so I can see that ass."

"What's with you girls these days? First, one kisses me and offers me dinner, and now you're jockeying to see my backside?"

She laughed. "No worries. I'm not in the market, but there's nothing wrong with a little window shopping." On the table in front of her were several pieces of paper. From a distance, it seemed like she was creating a to-do list, but Merrick was trained to pay attention. On the pages were lists all right, but not stuff she needed to do. The one closest to him had the heading "grossest food to eat." She put a column from A to Z and started with Anchovies.

"You don't like anchovies? Can't have a good Caesar salad without them."

"No small canned or jarred fish for me."

She didn't look like the small-town type. She was more *Housewives of Orange County* meets cast member of *Survivor*. Definitely out of her element in Aspen Cove, but then again, so was he.

He wiped the bottle's condensation from his hand on his pants and held it out. "I'm Merrick, by the way, and you're?"

"I'm JJ ... Jewel. I'm Jewel Monroe."

She was as much of a misfit as he was with her Hollywood looks and witness protection persona. She'd been hiding in Aspen Cove for a few weeks trying to blend in, but Jewel Monroe wasn't someone that went unnoticed. There was a story to this girl, but he wasn't sure he had time to figure it out.

"What brings you to Aspen Cove?"

"My Porsche Cayenne."

Yep, there was a story there, but it would have to wait for another day. This one would need some interrogating. He plopped a five on the counter. She rang up his water and made change. "I'll catch you later, Jewel."

"I'll be here, Merrick. Enjoy your pizza and beer."

That woman was one to watch. She paid attention, not that the whole scene unfolding in her store didn't draw it.

Now that he was officially off duty, he needed a beer. Across the street and a few doors down was Bishop's Brewhouse. On his way, he stopped at his truck and took off his khaki uniform shirt, trading it for a navy-blue polo. He figured he had enough time to drink a beer before heading home for a quick shower.

He entered and found Doc sitting at the bar. He'd taken a liking to the older man who passed out advice like a therapist—one who didn't charge hundreds for each session.

"Merrick, my son. How are you settling in?"

His reference to the word son always made Merrick feel welcome. His father had abandoned them when he was five, which forced Merrick to grow up fast. He always felt responsible for his mother and sister.

"I've made the move and adjusted without much trouble." He was happy to be out of the city. Denver had grown big, and the problems too many.

"We're happy to have you here in our tiny town."

Cannon walked in from the back room and grinned. "I hear you've got a hot date tonight."

Merrick rolled his eyes. "News travels faster here than a bank robber's getaway car." He pointed to Doc's half-full mug and raised a finger. "I'll have one of those, please."

Cannon took a frosted mug from below the counter and pulled the tap. "Sage was there when Deanna came into the bakery. She stopped by for one of my grade-A kisses before going home. She mentioned it." He slid the mug to Merrick.

After a long draw, he licked the foam off his lips. "It all happened so fast. I don't know how I went from investigating an argument to kissing Deanna and saying yes to a date."

Doc chuckled. "Listen here, son."

Cannon reached over and patted Merrick's shoulder. "Looks like you're getting a mentoring session. I'll be in the back if you need me."

Merrick never had a mentor. He didn't know if he should be flattered or flustered. One thing was certain, and that was his mother had taught him to be respectful, so if Doc wanted to give him words of wisdom, he'd happily listen.

"I'm all ears, Doc."

"Let me tell you about the women in this town."

Doc gulped his beer like he needed the alcohol for reinforcement. "They are all strong and independent. They may want a man, but they don't need one, and if someone has set her eyes on you, then you're one lucky SOB."

"I'm not sure she chose me exactly. If I had to guess, I was convenient."

"Why'd you say yes, then?"

That was a question to ponder. Deanna was pretty with her honey-colored hair and brown eyes, but he met many pretty girls. If he had to take an honest guess, it would be that he didn't like the vibe he was getting from her. That asshole Red had hurt her feelings, and he had a soft spot for tender-hearted women.

"I wasn't fond of the way Red was talking to her like she didn't matter."

Doc smiled. "Some men don't ever take the time to really see a woman past her assets. You were looking at her heart and soul first."

Merrick gulped his beer. "In truth, Doc. I saw her assets too, but they weren't a motivator."

Doc scowled, which pulled his mustache down on both corners. "You don't think she's pretty?"

He shook his head. "What I mean is, while she's pretty, I was more concerned with her safety than her sex appeal."

He ran his finger down the mug, sending the

condensation to the bar. "I'm not all up on what's hot these days. Damn people are piercing their noses, ears, and lips like they didn't have enough holes. Then there are the ones who color everything from their hair to their skin." Doc snorted. "A few years ago, one of the bikers waddled into my clinic. And when I say waddled, I mean walking like he'd been on a horse for a week without a break. He whipped off his pants and pointed to his pecker, which was huge. Not naturally huge, but swollen and red and hot. The damn idiot had pierced his penis and got an infection. That thing was worse than getting the clap. The treatment is the same, but holy hell, man, who sticks a barbell on the end of their pecker?"

Merrick rubbed the stubble on his chin. "Is there a lesson to this?"

Doc nodded. "Stick with the holes you were born with. Nature knows best."

"Got it." He sipped his beer and watched the last of the foam bubbles burst, leaving behind liquid gold.

"Now back to the women of Aspen Cove. I met my Phyllis here in town when we were youngsters. At that time, I was the fisherman, and she was the trout. I cast my line, and on the hook, I offered my love, commitment, and anything else I had, which wasn't much more than a prize hog at the time, but Phyllis was the first love of my life."

Doc stared off into space as if he was reliving a moment and then shook his head and turned back to Merrick.

"Now, my Agatha is a different story. I'd had a grand love and lost her. I wasn't looking for anyone, and happy to live out my life in peace. Women don't bring you peace, son. They bring you everything else from happiness to hurt, but rarely peace. When it came to Agatha, she was the fox, and I was the rabbit. I tried to outrun her, but she was too cunning and too fast. I love that woman differently than Phyllis, but no less. We are in a different phase of our lives, and she's perfect for me now. Maybe Deanna is who you should be with in this phase of your life."

Merrick shook his head. If Doc shaved and put on a long red wig and slapped on some lipstick, he sounded just like his mother. She was always trying to fix him up with someone or another. He'd passed thirty-five, and her grandmother's clock was ticking.

"I'm not ready to put a ring on her finger. I'm just having pizza and beer."

Doc took a five from his wallet and laid it on top of a napkin riddled with tic-tac-toe. The Os appeared to have won.

"That's how it all starts. You have a meal and a

drink. You lock lips and then bodies. Pretty soon, I'll be marrying you on Cannon's dock at sunset. It's the way it works, my boy." Doc slid off the barstool and stood still for a minute. He shifted his legs and then his hips. "Old bones need to settle in place before I move them."

Merrick pulled the five off the napkin and handed it back to Doc. "I've got your beer. It's the least I can do to pay for your timely advice." He pulled out his wallet and tossed a ten and a five on the counter.

"I didn't give you advice, son."

Merrick finished his beer and slid off the stool. "Sure, you did. You told me not to pierce my pecker."

"I told you more than that." He shuffled toward the door with Merrick following closely. "Here's another piece of advice. Bring flowers and wear cologne. Women like that." He sniffed the air. "If you don't have any, I've got that Old Spice in the pharmacy."

"I'm good on the cologne. Good advice on the flowers." He pivoted and headed back to the Corner Store.

"Glad I could help," Doc called after him. "I'll be in Bishop's Brewhouse tomorrow for that next beer you owe me."

CHAPTER THREE

Deanna rushed around, making sure everything was picked up. She fluffed the pillows on her couch and moved the corner chair to hide the spot where the wood was warped. She didn't have the budget the others had to refurbish her old worn-out house. As Samantha's assistant, she made decent money, but she didn't get the big bucks like the artists did.

Her stipend to move to Aspen Cove was generous, but she prudently put some in savings and took a chunk to help pay for her sister Delia's divorce. One thing about the Archer women, they were terrible at picking men. Maybe it was because their mother gave them all D names. Deanna was the oldest, followed by Delia, and ending with Demi. Her mother might have been better off calling them

Disaster One, Two, and Three since they'd all failed at love.

"This isn't a real date." She glanced at Sherman, who curled up at the corner of the couch, looking at her like she'd lost her mind. "I mean, he probably thinks it's a date, but I'll set him straight right away."

Her poodle buried his head behind his paws like he was embarrassed.

"Why are you hiding your face?" She reorganized the books on her coffee table. They were all poetry. Some were about love at its best, but most were about love lost. "I kissed him. Not the kind of little peck you give your mom after Sunday dinner, but the type of kiss that lands you naked between the sheets."

She fanned her heated face with one of the books and set it on top of the others.

How was it she reacted so strongly to the kiss when she didn't know the man? That had to be part of the allure. He was like a forbidden fruit. A rich candy truffle she snuck while on a diet.

A look at the clock said time was wasting. She had maybe ten minutes before he arrived. Did she stay in her jeans and T-shirt, or did she change into something nicer?

"This isn't a date!" Sherman hated it when she raised her voice. It didn't happen often, and that's why he got so upset. He jumped from the sofa and piddled on the floor. "Seriously?"

He looked at her with a what-did-you-expect expression.

She hurriedly cleaned up the mess and raced to her bedroom to change. She could hear her mother's voice in her head. *In for a penny, in for a pound.*

She chose a green sundress that complimented her eyes and slipped on a pair of sandals. That was all she was doing for this non-date. When she looked in the mirror, she realized she hadn't touched up her makeup, so she moved toward the bathroom and primped just enough to look decent. That was all she was doing for this event. As she turned to walk out the door, she spritzed on her perfume. Okay, now that's all she was doing—nothing more.

She preheated the oven to cook the pizza and pulled down her favorite dishes, one's she'd inherited from her grandmother. There weren't many opportunities to use them, so her non-date seemed the perfect occasion.

When she heard the sound of a car door closing, her heart took off like a squirrel avoiding an owl. It banked left and right in her chest until it found a steadier pace that didn't make her head spin.

Sherman was already at the door. Dogs had the

most sensitive hearing unless, of course, you were calling them, and then they were deaf.

"Be nice," she told her stubborn poodle. Sherman didn't like anyone, especially Red. The poor man had been bitten by her poodle a few times. She had to give him credit, though, because he never gave up trying to pet him. Was that commitment or stupidity? At this point, she wasn't sure. All she knew was Sherman wasn't a fan. Maybe that should be her litmus test for dating. If they couldn't pass the Sherman test, then they were out.

A light tap on the door sent the poodle into a full-on big dog bark. It always cracked her up to see how protective he was for a fifteen-pound ball of fur.

She pointed to his bed. "Go lay down."

If a dog could look dejected, Sherman did, and he dragged himself slowly to his timeout space.

When she opened the door, she found Merrick standing on her porch with a bottle of wine and a bouquet. Her heart rate picked up its pace again, only this time, it wasn't running for cover but jumping for joy. This was the first time a man bought her flowers and offered them in person. Red left them on the porch to wither and die.

He looked at his offerings and held them out to her. "For you."

Was that a blush she saw rise to his cheeks?

"Thank you. They're beautiful." She took the flowers and wine and stood to the side. "Come in." As he passed through the door, she got a glimpse of her overgrown front yard. "I hope you didn't have trouble finding the front door. I wish I could grow something other than weeds. I fear it might be years before my house looks presentable."

"Houses take time ... and money." He glanced at his shoes. "Would you like me to take them off?"

A laugh bubbled up inside her. "No, there's nothing you can do to damage this floor that the last 80 years of residents haven't done already. My place is an eyesore, but I'm working on it."

She looked at her house through a stranger's eyes. It was a dump, but a warm, inviting one with overstuffed furniture that hugged her body each night she tucked into her favorite chair to read a book.

He stepped inside and looked around. "I love these old houses. What do you think they'd say if they had a voice?"

She closed the door behind him and moved toward the galley kitchen.

"Mine would say, *Sucker*. I love them too, but old homes are a money pit."

"Don't I know it. Luckily for me, I bought mine from Wes, and he gave me a remodeling allowance."

"I'm jealous. I purchased mine from Mason

Van der Veen, and he offered me nothing." She pulled out a jelly jar, from beneath the counter, for the flowers. "Thank you for these. They're beautiful."

"My mom taught me never to go anywhere empty-handed."

He leaned against the counter while she trimmed the stems and placed them in the water.

"I got the same lesson. It was part of a trilogy that went something like, *Never show up anywhere empty-handed. Kindness is key. And your attitude is always a choice.* My mom was a Gandhi of her time." Happy with how the flowers looked, she walked them to the table and set them in the center. "Let me pop the pizza in the oven. Make yourself at home." She pulled out a chair for him. "Beer or the wine you brought?"

"I'll take a beer, please. Not sure about the wine. It was something new Jewel added to her lineup at the Corner Store. I picked it up with the flowers."

Deanna pulled Dalton's take-and-bake pizza from her refrigerator and placed it on a stone. She was a sucker for home parties. She had entire collections of Pampered Chef, Scentsy, and Tupperware. She was sure there was a rehab for home-party shoppers and she probably needed a thirty-day stint at one.

"What do you think about her?"

The chair creaked when he sat. She hoped that his big frame didn't snap the legs.

"Jewel?"

"Yes, I hear she's new in town too. There are a lot of us newbies."

"I haven't had a chance to get to know her. It seems like an odd career choice for a woman who drives a Porsche, but who am I to judge. I moved here too."

Once the pizza was in the oven, she took two beers from the refrigerator and joined him at the table.

"Why did you move to Aspen Cove?" She failed to twist the top off and handed him the bottles. "Would you mind?"

His muscles barely flexed as he uncapped the beers and handed one back to her. "Cheers," he said. "Here's to our first date."

Oh, hell. He did think this was a date.

"About that. I feel like I duped you into this dinner."

He took a sip of his beer. When he put the bottle down, he looked at her with eyes that seemed to sparkle with delight. "I realize it was unorthodox, but hey, it works." The corners of his lips turned up into a grin. "If it all works out, I can have a ring on your finger by next week."

She was mid-sip and choked on the trickle of beer that managed to make it into her mouth. "What?"

"I'm razzing you. I know what this is, but I figured that we could get to know each other while we're here. Nothing wrong with two new people in town becoming friends."

Relief flooded her, followed by a weird sense of disappointment. "I'd like that. Now tell me why you're in Aspen Cove."

He leaned back against the spindles of her antique chair. When they didn't splinter, she thanked the spirits who'd made the pieces so durable and strong.

"Law enforcement is tough and dangerous. The last time I ended up in a gun battle was the last. While crime has no address, I don't think hardcore criminals have found their way to Aspen Cove."

She leaned in. "Have you ever been shot?"

He pulled up the sleeve of his T-shirt to show an angry-looking red scar near his shoulder. "I took one here. Luckily, it only grazed bone and muscle. It was a wake-up call, though. I love serving and protecting, and I don't have a problem putting myself in the line of fire to save someone, but Denver didn't pay me enough to die."

She reached forward to skim her fingers over the almost-healed wound. "Did it hurt bad?"

He leaned forward so she could reach more easily. The raised scar was soft and velvety. His skin was warm—almost hot.

"The only way I can think to describe it is being burned from the inside out. It felt like getting stabbed with a red-hot poker."

"I can't imagine. The most dangerous part of my job is not killing Red. I've only gone as far as lobbing a muffin at his head."

He stroked his chin, where his finely trimmed beard framed his features. "What's with you two?"

"We dated, and it went badly, but ..." Dated was a stretch. She'd crushed on him for a long time. All it took was a little music and a glass of wine for her to cave in to her baser needs and a second's afterthought for him to pull away. The truth hurt. Her heart felt pierced by a flaming blade.

"Are you done with him or trying to win him back?"

She almost felt ashamed to sit here with Merrick, who was obviously one of the good guys. "You know how it goes. You can think with your head or your heart."

"Which one is talking to you these days?" He picked at the softened label and pulled it off in one piece.

"I stopped listening to my heart long ago. I'm certain I've got faulty wiring. Right now, I'm using my head, and it keeps telling me not to give up. I've got a lot of time invested in this relationship. It's kind of like saving a bunch of money and then tossing it away."

"I can see that, but at some point, you have to be honest with yourself. Some investments aren't good long term. You get in and get out and move on. The dividend is what you take away. Let's go back to my job. At what point is the risk no longer worth the reward?"

"That is something I'll have to decide."

"Only you can. Until then, I'm happy to eat your pizza and drink your beer."

The timer went off, and Deanna brought their dinner and plates to the table. "Thank you, Merrick. I probably should apologize for accosting you in the Corner Store, and thank you for not arresting me for sexual assault."

He grabbed a slice and set it on the plate. "Though it was a surprise at first, I quickly became a willing accomplice. If Red can't appreciate the level of perfection in your kisses, he's an idiot."

"Perfection?" Her insides heated at his words. She loved to kiss and thought she was decent at it, but perfection? "You enjoyed our lip-lock?"

He pulled his lower lip between his teeth in the most seductive way. If this weren't a pretend date, she would have gladly offered him another sample, but he wasn't who she wanted. She wanted Red.

"I definitely enjoyed it, but I understand where you're coming from."

"Ah," she said. "You have some unrequited love situation you want to tell me about?"

He laughed. It was a full rolling belly laugh that came from his soul.

"Nope, I generally get what I want too. However, according to my mother, I'm getting on in years, and if I don't find a wife, I'm sure she'll order me one."

"Her grandmother's biological clock is ticking, huh? Thankfully, my sister Demi, the youngest of my siblings, gave my mother a granddaughter a few years ago. Otherwise, I'm sure Mom would be selling me off to the highest bidder." She covered her mouth to suppress a giggle. "Scratch that, she'd probably pay someone to marry me and give her a grandchild."

He lifted his bottle of beer again. "Let's toast to meddling mothers and friends who know what that feels like."

With a click of their bottles, they drank and enjoyed their pizza.

The next hour was spent talking, and after a dessert of gooey caramel brownies, she walked Merrick to the door to say goodbye.

"I had a nice time," he leaned over and kissed her on the cheek.

"Me too. Thank you for being a good sport."

He tapped his chest. "Protect and serve. That's what I do."

She giggled. "You went above and beyond the call of duty."

He took a step back. "Happy to help, but ... can I say one thing?"

She nodded. "Yes."

"You deserve more."

As she closed the door, she wondered if he was right.

CHAPTER FOUR

The next morning Merrick stood in front of the mirror shaving. He wasn't feeling particularly rested as his thoughts went to Deanna all night long. Was it the initial kiss that short-wired his brain, or was it his protective mechanisms that made him want to shield her from hurt? Either way, he had to let it go. She wasn't the girl for him. She was head and heart set on Red, and it wouldn't serve him well to fall for a woman who could never give herself fully. In his mind, a person deserved to be loved completely or not at all.

His phone, sitting on the bathroom counter, lit up and vibrated itself off the edge, toppling toward the floor. He caught it mid-fall.

"Hello, Mom." She was the only one who called

him before his shift. Elsa Buchanan was one of those women who never seemed to sleep. Maybe it was a habit that came from being a single mom. She was up before the kids and went to bed after them.

"Hello, sweetheart. How's my boy today?"

Funny how at thirty-five, she still considered him her boy. "I'm good, just getting ready to go to work."

"How is Aspen Cove?" Silence filled the phone for a long second. "Are you enjoying your life there thus far?"

"Still adjusting, but all is good." He left the bathroom and walked to the kitchen where his coffeepot was finishing its brew cycle. "You should come for a visit sometime."

"That's why I'm calling. I thought maybe on your next day off, I could come up and have lunch with you."

His mother's love made him warm from the inside out. She was always so attentive and put her kids first in all things. "That would be great. Are you sure you only want to come for lunch? I have an extra room you can sleep in if you want to stay a day or two."

"While that sounds lovely, I have work as well. With school back in session, there's too much stuff to get done and too few hours to finish it in. Are you off Saturday?"

As it turned out, he was. His mother had this sixth sense about him and time. "As a matter of fact, I am. We rotate shifts, so everyone gets at least one weekend day a month, and this Saturday is mine."

"That's perfect. Do you mind if I bring a friend?"

The warning bells went off. "Would this friend happen to be a new teacher who is single?" His mother was relentless in the matchmaking department. As the librarian for a Denver elementary school, Mom met all the eligible teachers. She considered women in a field that catered to children's education and well-being the best pool for wives since they were kid-centric.

"Sandra is a lovely woman. She's still in her childbearing prime at twenty-nine and looking for a solid man to build a life with."

"Mom, while I appreciate your zealous nature, don't you think the logistics of a three-hour commute for dates would be a nightmare?"

"Well, it's not ideal, but there are plenty of smaller towns closer to Denver that you could have looked into. Take Elizabeth, or Franktown, or Parker for that matter."

He let out an exaggerated sigh. "I did, and I chose Aspen Cove."

"Are there any women there? It couldn't hurt to

meet Sandra. She's quite pretty, and she cooks a mean brownie."

At the mention of brownies, he thought about Deanna and the caramel turtle deliciousness she served him last night. While she didn't make them herself, she had excellent taste in sweets.

The only way his mom wasn't bringing Sandra was if he already had a girlfriend.

"Listen, Mom, come up for lunch but don't bring Sandra."

"Why not?" He heard the frustration in her voice. "You know, Merrick, you're not getting any younger. Love will never find you if you don't open your heart and mind to the idea that you're lovable."

He burst out laughing. "I know I'm lovable. That's not the issue." He had to get to work and needed an out that wouldn't create an hour-long lecture from his mother. The problem with librarians was they were readers, and readers liked words. His mother could be quite talkative when she wanted to get her point across.

"Then what's the problem?"

"I have a girlfriend, and I'm fairly certain she wouldn't be happy if you tried to set me up with someone else."

He pulled the phone from his ear when his mother squealed. "Why didn't you tell me?"

His mind raced to come up with something believable. "It's all very new."

"What's her name?"

"Deanna," he blurted.

He hated to lie to her. He prided himself on being an honest and trustworthy man, but if he didn't give his mom a name, he'd be in a relationship with Sandra. And while she was probably a lovely woman, he wasn't ready or willing to trade in his life again for a new location and experience. He rather liked the laid-back pace of small-town living. Aspen Cove fit him like a comfortable pair of shoes.

"I can't wait to meet her on Saturday."

"Well, I'll have to see if she's available."

His mother snorted. "Why wouldn't she be? It's Saturday, and any woman with her eye on my boy will want to meet his mother. You know what they say ..."

"What do they say, Mom?"

"How a man treats his mother is how he'll treat his wife."

"Don't reserve the church yet. We just started seeing each other."

"We'll see," his mother said with a trill that could only mean trouble. "See you Saturday. Can't wait to meet your girl."

She hung up before he could say another word.

He poured himself a cup of coffee and walked

into the living room. Looking at his house, he realized his life was as compartmentalized as his home. Baxter tried to persuade him to tear down the walls to his kitchen to open things up. Was his home a metaphor for his life? Everything had its own little space. He boxed up his relationships and didn't let them intersect with his family life. It wasn't as if he hadn't dated, but the first few times he brought girls home to meet Mom, she had them married and producing grandchildren in record time. Then his last long-term relationship ended because she couldn't handle the risks inherent to him being a cop.

He moved farther into the living room, convinced that divided spaces were safer for everyone. But how could he keep Deanna in her space while temporarily wanting her in his?

He finished his coffee and left for work.

When he arrived at the sheriff's office, he found his boss, Aiden Cooper, sitting at his desk, scrubbing the word "Daddy" from the top.

"Marking her territory?"

Aiden chuckled. "No, just Kellyn trying to teach her brother how to spell." He sprayed the desktop once more and gave it a final swipe. "Could be worse. She could have started with some unsavory words she's been picking up from school like butthead and asshole."

"Out of the mouths of babes." Merrick sat in the chair in front of Aiden's desk. "Do you have anything you need me to do?"

Aiden shook his head. "Not really. Paperwork is caught up. The only exciting thing that happened since yesterday was that Mrs. Brown's cat went missing, but he was easy to find, seeing as how she'd dressed him in a clown costume. He was hiding out behind the bakery. I'd hide too if I had to wear some of the outfits she puts him in."

Merrick had caught a glimpse or two of the poor animal. Last week he found him skulking around the alley wearing a fish head hat. That gave new meaning to catfish.

"Mrs. Brown needs to find a man. At least she hasn't set her sights on you yet. Poor Mark got a lot of attention when he became the deputy. She asked for him by name. Then again, I heard you have a girlfriend, and as fast as gossip travels through town, maybe Mrs. Brown has heard the rumors too. What's this about you and Deanna?"

"Just a rumor. Nothing is going on with her. She was trying to make that guy Red jealous, so she asked me over to dinner."

"Do you like her?"

"It doesn't matter if I do or not. She has set her

sights on someone else. I'm always a day late and a dollar short."

Aiden eyed him for a second. "They say that nice guys always finish last, but that's not a bad thing. Taking your time with someone means you get to know them. Marina held me off with a ten-foot pole for the longest time. In the end, I finished, and it sure doesn't feel like last place to me."

Merrick had seen how in love his boss was with Marina and vice versa. He'd heard little bits of their story and knew they'd run the gauntlet to be together.

"It's not like that for us. I find her attractive. I mean, come on, have you seen her? But, I'm not investing my time into a relationship with someone who wants someone else."

"Maybe she only thinks she wants him. Spend some time with her. There's got to be a reason you two can get together that's not a date."

Merrick shook his head. It was as if the universe was conspiring against him. "There is one." A growl escaped his throat before he could swallow it. "My mother is coming to town, and if I don't look like I'm with someone, she'll bring me a bride. Maybe hanging out with Deanna can serve us both. I can make that idiot jealous, and she can keep my match-making mother at bay."

"Be careful," Aiden warned. "You might just fall for her."

Merrick rose from the chair. "Unlikely. She's not meant for me, but she's too good for that guy." He walked to the door. "I'm going to make the rounds." By that, he meant he was heading to Deanna's to negotiate.

CHAPTER FIVE

He traded his truck for the marked cruiser. He wasn't going anywhere in a professional capacity, but he was on shift, and if needed, he'd be ready.

He drove down Main Street, which was always quiet unless the weekend tourists got a little rowdy. So far, he'd only had issues with the groupies. Who knew women could be such trouble? At least now he didn't have to rescue Alex. There weren't many women sneaking into his place since he fell in love with Mercy.

He wound his way through streets like Hyacinth and Jasmine until he came to Daisy Lane. The street seemed fitting for a woman like Deanna. In some ways, she reminded him of a daisy with her golden hair and brown eyes.

Outside her worn bungalow, he took several breaths. He wasn't generally the nervous type, but he'd never propositioned a woman in this way. Sure, he'd done plenty of propositioning in his days, but it never started with "Hey, babe. Let's say you and I fake a relationship. I'll help you get that good for nothing idiot back if you help me avoid my mother's matchmaking attempts by being my fake girlfriend." Nope, this was a first.

He walked several steps toward her entry and then turned around and headed back to his cruiser, thinking how insane the situation was. He did this several times, talking himself into the ruse and out of it. Nothing good ever came out of deceit in his experience, but he wasn't ready to let his mother hitch his wagon to some teacher's star.

As he started his fourth trek to her front door, it opened. Standing in front of him was Deanna, dressed in shorts and a T-shirt that said *All I need is mascara and caffeine.*

"You coming in, or do you have a step count to meet before you knock?"

A poodle bolted past her and raced toward him. Merrick wasn't sure if he was in for a greeting or an ankle nipping. The night before, the poodle kept his distance, but he was vigilant. He watched every move Merrick made.

"You got coffee?" He bent over and picked up

the dog. When he stood, he was greeted by a shocked expression. "What?"

Deanna shook her head. "Sherman doesn't warm up to new people easily. I'm surprised, is all."

"All people or some people?" He hugged the dog to his chest and nuzzled his chin into the curly coat of fur. Sherman rose above his trimmed beard and licked his face.

"He doesn't like Red." She waved him forward and stood to the side of the door so he could enter.

"I once heard that dogs and babies were good judges of character."

She led him into the kitchen, where she took two mugs from the cupboard and poured them both a cup of coffee. "I was always told you shouldn't judge a book by its cover."

He gave Sherman a final pet and put him on the floor. "Not true. A book cover can tell you everything about what's inside, and if it doesn't, then you've been duped."

"Bibliophile?"

He took the coffee she offered. "I'd rather read the book than see the movie."

"Read any Nicholas Sparks lately?"

He nearly choked. "I wouldn't say he's my go-to for material, but I've read a few."

She pointed to the table and took the same seat she did the night before. "I'm calling bullshit."

He sat and stared at her while he rolled through the titles he'd read, then he tapped his chest. "I'm wounded that you think I'd lie. As a matter of fact, the last Sparks book I read was *Safe Haven*, but I've also read *The Notebook* and *A Walk to Remember*, which nearly gutted me. Remember, I grew up in a houseful of women, and they influenced which books were on the shelves. Two against one is a majority."

She reached over and touched his hand. "You poor baby." It was a soft touch that radiated heat across his skin. He was almost certain it was from her holding her mug, but he couldn't be sure. "How did you ever survive?"

"You go with what you know. I think growing up under a woman's influence has helped me be a better man."

"How so?"

He shrugged. "I don't blush when I have to run to the store to buy feminine products. I know the difference between lipstick and lip pencil and understand why both are important. I've been through enough bouts of PMS and heartbreaks to have insight into how tough women have it and how strong they are to deal with knuckleheads like us men."

She stared at him for a moment and then nodded her head. "So, you're basically a girl with a penis."

His head shook vigorously. "Noooo, all I'm saying is that to be a good partner to a woman, you have to stand in her stilettos for a day. Not literally, but figuratively. Having been raised by a single mother and having a sister gave me insight into how women feel and think, and I believe that helps me be more aware as a man."

She patted his hand and drew hers back. "I like that you think so, but seeing is believing." She sipped her coffee and set her mug back on the table. "Tell me, were you just in the neighborhood, or did I do something nefarious like park my car and not turn my wheels to the curb?"

He liked her quick wit. She had a sharp tongue, but that meant she had a fire in her, and he enjoyed a woman with passion.

He sat for a minute, thinking about how to broach the subject of a mutual agreement. The tapping of his fingers on the wooden table filled the silence.

"Do you want to pace the walkway again for a few minutes?" Her shoulders set with seriousness, but her eyes danced with merriment.

"No, I'm just trying to figure out how to word what I have to say, so it comes out right." He picked up his mug and downed his remaining coffee.

"A man who thinks before he speaks. You *were* raised by women." She leaned back with a smug smile on her face. "Blurt it out. I work with Troglodytes, so I'm used to all the grunting and chest pounding."

"I've tucked my caveman away for now. He only comes out when I'm threatened or jealous or around Red because I'm not really a fan." When she opened her mouth to speak, he held up his hand. "I know you like him, and you want him, which is why I'm here. I have a proposition for you."

"Ooh, now that sounds like fun."

She wiggled in her seat, and everything about it was alluring. Something told him this was a bad idea, but what other choice did he have? He stuck his foot in his mouth with his mother, and Deanna was the only one who could help him pull it out.

He took two breaths. One for cleansing and one for courage. "I need a fake girlfriend, and in return, I'll do whatever you need that's legal to make Red jealous." He shrugged.

"I guess ticketing him for breathing is out of the question?"

He considered that for a second. It might be fun ticketing Red for minor infractions like jaywalking. It wasn't something they did in Aspen Cove, but karma was a bitch named Merrick.

"Do they honestly ticket you in California for not turning your wheels to the curb?"

47

She sighed and nodded. "Yes, and it's total BS because I didn't even live on a hill. I get it if you're on an incline, but my car wasn't going anywhere."

He understood the policy and the safety factor, but there were so many more important things to focus on than minor traffic violations. Unless ... you were an asshole named Red.

"About my proposition? What do you think?"

"I need more details. How long are we talking, and who are you trying to fool?"

"I think I'll be good for a weekend, but I'll default to your needs."

"A man who cares about my needs—shocking." She pulled her hair from her ponytail and let the strands fall over her shoulder. Something florally like the scent of lavender wafted through the air.

"If your needs aren't being met, you're looking at the wrong man." He lifted his brows in a challenge.

"You're probably right, but you know ... every girl loves a bad boy."

"Until she's visiting him in jail and applying for conjugal dates."

Her nose scrunched up. "Ick, I thought that was only in the movies?"

"Nope. It happens, but it depends on the prison and the behavior of the inmates."

She shivered and laid her palms flat on the table. "Enough about bad boys. Tell me why you need me?"

He explained about his mother's threat to bring a "friend" and how he'd blurted out her name.

"Do you think she'll see me as a perfect match?"

"You're a woman of childbearing years. That's all she'll care about."

"Ooh, high standards."

He stood and took his mug to the sink.

"Is that a yes or a no?"

"Do I have to kiss you?"

He spun around to face her. "Was the first time that bad?"

She pulled her lower lip between her teeth, which was so damn sexy that he had to turn away.

"No, that's the problem. The kiss was good. It could be a distraction. You know, like chocolate. It's really good, but if you eat too much, it's bad news."

He turned back to look at her. "You don't have to kiss me unless you want to."

"Do I have to cook for your mom?"

That would be a fantastic idea. "Can you cook?"

"Does a bird have feathers?"

He moved toward her. "If you're cooking chicken, I'd prefer it to be plucked. I'm pretty sure my mom would like that too."

"Okay, so I'm cooking, but you're buying the food."

"Deal." He offered her his hand to shake on it.

"Are we doing this?"

"It would seem so. Let's shake on it."

Her palm fit inside his, and within seconds, they had a deal.

"When will you need me?" he asked.

"How about Wednesday night at Bishop's Brewhouse? It's karaoke night, and the band is always there. I'll buy."

"Not a chance, babe. I'm an old-fashioned guy, and my woman never pays."

"Are we starting already? If that's the case, then I'll drink top-shelf."

She was a sassy one. This could be fun.

"Only the best for you."

"Is babe what you're going to call me?"

He had no idea. It just came out and felt natural.

"Is it a problem?"

"No, I've never had a nickname. I guess babe is good. Is there anything I should call you?"

"Anything but asshole is fine."

"Okay, sweetie." She stood and moved toward the coffeepot. "You want another cup, love?" Her voice softened on the term of endearment.

"I like that one, and no, I have to get to work so I can afford to pay for your top-shelf liquor."

She kicked up a heel and giggled. "I'm not cheap or easy ... well, maybe I'm one or both. I'm a bit confused these days."

He followed her to the door. "Don't ever let anyone else define who you are. Be you."

She almost wilted in front of him.

"What if being me isn't enough?"

He lowered himself a few inches until they were eye to eye. "Anyone who doesn't see your value isn't worth your time." He kissed her forehead and opened the front door. "See you later, babe."

"Wednesday at six, love. Don't be late."

"And keep you waiting? Never." He walked to the cruiser with a lightness a big man shouldn't feel. It was as if he were floating. This fake relationship might be the best one he'd ever had.

CHAPTER SIX

Deanna stared at the pile of clothes on the bed. She was sure a dress and heels were far too fancy for Bishop's Brewhouse, but she had nice legs and wanted to show them off.

Her nerves itched on the inside. Somehow things had gotten muddled in her brain. She was going on a fake date with Merrick, to try to win back Red, but she had to keep reminding herself that it wasn't the real deal with the handsome deputy sheriff. Her eyes had to stay on the prize.

She picked up her tattered jeans, the ones she paid more for to have holes in them. Stepping into them, she tugged them over her thighs—maybe she should stop with the muffins and brownies. Was that why Red dropped her like a hot brick?

She moved toward the full-length mirror, hopping into her jeans until she got there. She turned and looked over her shoulder to stare at her bottom.

"I've seen worse." She'd seen him with worse. Maybe that was it. She was smack dab in the middle of average. She had an ass that fell somewhere in between Kardashian and Kunis.

She moved back to the bed and selected an off-the-shoulder tunic. One last look in the mirror confirmed that she wasn't trying too hard. No doubt, she'd blend in with all the locals and pale in comparison to the groupies.

"Ugh ... the groupies." They came out of the woodwork on Wednesdays to drive to Aspen Cove. Bishop's Brewhouse made a killing on hump day.

Once she checked her makeup for a final time and slicked on her favorite mango flavored lip gloss, she was out the door. She debated between driving and walking and finally decided to walk. If Merrick was buying, she was drinking, and alcohol and cars were never a good mix.

Walking through her mostly empty neighborhood, she took in the old, vacant bungalows and tried to picture a time when the street was bustling with activity. When small children played ball in the yard and mothers in pretty floral dresses brought them lemonade and cookies. Aspen Cove was picture-perfect now, even in its abandonment; she couldn't imagine what it was back then.

As she turned toward Main Street, she caught a glimpse of Merrick walking into the bar. He was hard to miss with his height. Not that Red was a small man at nearly six feet tall, but those extra inches Merrick had on him made him look bigger than life. At five foot eight, she used to be the tall girl, but standing next to the new deputy made her feel downright petite.

Just as she gripped the handle to open the door, a large hand covered hers. She swung around to find Red tucked up close behind her.

"Can we talk?" he asked.

Her first instinct was to melt and say yes, but she knew better than to give in so easily. That was her problem. She'd been a doormat for the man for years by catering to his needs and making sure that anything Red wanted, Red got, but no more.

"I wish I could, but I've got a date."

His eyes grew wide. "With that asshat?"

"I'm not sure who you're referring to, but my date is with Merrick." She heaved a sigh and smiled broadly. "He's such an honorable man." With a tug, she pulled the door open and walked inside, leaving Red on the threshold.

In the darkened bar, she searched for her fake boyfriend and found him at the bar ordering drinks.

He spotted her immediately and looked at her the way she had dreamed Red would. Merrick took her in slowly like he was savoring the sight of her. The door opened behind her, and Red walked in. She didn't need to turn to see it was him. She could tell by the way Merrick's jaw ticked.

"Hey, babe." He rushed toward her and wrapped his arms around her like he hadn't seen her in a lifetime when it had only been a few days. His lips brushed the top of her head, so naturally, she felt like this was her everyday life. "I ordered you a beer, but if you'd like a wine or a mixed drink, I'm happy to change the order."

She tilted her head back to look into his eyes. "Beer is great. If I have wine, I'm guaranteed to make poor choices."

Merrick quirked a brow. Some men had stoic faces that didn't show emotion. She was certain Merrick could put on a poker face as effective as any man, given he was in law enforcement and most likely trained to shutter his emotions, but when he was off duty and let down his guard, his face showed everything. Right now, he had questions about wine and poor choices.

"We all choose poorly from time to time. One bad decision isn't the equivalent of a string of them."

"Sounds like there's a story to tell. Let's get our

beers, and I'm all ears." If she was going to play her part, she needed to know more about him. Mothers were tricky when it came to their kids. If Merrick's mom wanted him married and was picking out options, she'd want to make sure Deanna was the right fit. The right fit would need to know details about him. Details that only a real girlfriend would know.

Merrick grabbed their beers and led her over to a corner table. The bar wasn't packed yet, but by eight o'clock, it would be a mosh pit of bodies jockeying to see who the flavor of the night would be. Now with Alex off the market, there were only three single band members left. Red and Gray would definitely come to the bar tonight. Griffen Taylor, who just signed on, was in transition and moving from Denver to Aspen Cove to avoid the commute to the recording studio. She wasn't sure if he would show tonight or not.

"How has your week been?" Merrick pulled out her chair, and she took a seat with her back to the stage. She was sure he'd done that on purpose. To have her mad dogging Red wouldn't lead anyone to believe their relationship was credible.

"It was good. I found a house for Griffen, and I'm negotiating a fair price from that Van der Veen guy. He owns a lot of the properties in town."

"I haven't met him, but I've heard of him. His reputation isn't all that great."

"He's a businessman first, so if you speak his language, then he's all right. It's a good thing he's selling the properties and not renting them. I could see him as a slumlord if that was the case. He's the kind of guy that would tell you he's charging you more for rusty water because it's mineral-rich."

"How did you talk him into a fair deal, and who's Griffen?"

"Let's start with Griffen; he's the new keyboardist for the band. He's moving up from Denver."

Merrick nodded. "It's good to see the town growing." He lifted his beer. "Shall we toast to new beginnings?"

She picked up her mug and tapped his. "To new beginnings." Her head turned slightly to peek Red's way, but Merrick cupped her cheek.

"Don't look at him. I'll tell you everything. Right now, he's sitting at the end of the bar glaring at me. That's exactly what we want. Now tell me about Mason Van der Veen, and how you negotiated with a man like him?"

She could feel the heat of Red's stare on her back. She thought it would make her feel flattered, but all it made her feel was angry because he was treating her like a bone he abandoned, and now that another dog was interested, he wanted it back.

She took two more sips before she continued.

"Mason is a man motivated by money, so I spoke his language. One of the things I generally do well in my life is negotiate. I wouldn't be a good assistant to Samantha if I didn't. So, when he tried to blackball me on the price, I laid out the numbers. While Aspen Cove is growing, and there is a glut of vacant homes, many of them aren't occupancy ready."

"I would have thought that would make his bargaining power better."

"You would think, but it's fall, and that means the selling season here is on the waning edge. No one wants to buy a house that needs everything from flooring to insulation when the temperature drops. People who buy houses here are residents. The tourists move to places like Breckenridge or Estes Park and get their cute little seasonal cabins." She carved hieroglyphics in the side of the frost on the glass. "I told him he could sell today for x amount of dollars or hope that next year, he'd get the same."

"And he sold it to you?"

She nodded her head. "I can be quite persuasive when I need to be."

He leaned in, and she was confident he was going to kiss her.

"I bet you can," he whispered near her ear and pulled back, looking like he'd just won the lottery.

"I thought you were going to kiss me to make Red jealous."

Merrick pulled that full lower lip between his teeth. It was a gesture that made him look playful and sexy. Did he know that and use it to his advantage?

"I don't need to kiss you. He's already turning the color of his name."

"Really?"

"Yes, does that make you happy?"

Did it? This was what their agreement was about. He was helping her get Red back, and she was helping him avoid a maternal intervention.

"Yes, I suppose it does."

"Make sure, sweetheart, because it's about to get real, really fast."

She opened her mouth to ask what he meant, but before she could utter a word, he said, "You are so damn sexy, Deanna." He leaned over and kissed her. It started as a sweet lingering peck, but before she knew it, her arms wrapped around his neck, and somehow she was out of her chair and in Merrick's lap. Her lips parted, and their tongues met. His was velvety soft and tasted so sweet she was sure he was made of sugar. His lips were dreamy like pillows dipped in passion. When he pulled back, she was dizzy.

"He was on his way over. That was a diversion.

No man is going to come over and watch his woman kiss another man."

"Oh, right." It took her a second to get her bearings. She'd been kissed plenty in her thirty years but never once had a kiss made her lose her marbles like that.

She moved slowly from Merrick's lap and took her seat once again. A glance toward the bar showed a glowering Red. As soon as she stared his way, he pulled the girl standing next to him into his lap and covered her mouth with his. One thing was certain, that poor girl might be thrilled by the attention, but her toes weren't curling from that kiss. Another thing that bothered her was seeing him kiss the girl didn't bother her. That was something to consider.

"Is it hot in here?" She waved her hand in front of her face, and when that didn't work, she picked up her mug and pressed the cold, wet glass to her cheek.

"Hmm, hot?"

There went that lip between his teeth, and the inferno blazed again. She was losing her ever-loving mind. She wasn't here to fall for Merrick. He didn't want a girlfriend. In a roundabout way, he engaged her to avoid one. She needed to get her head in the game.

"Stop doing that with your lip. It's distracting.

Use that move on someone you want to melt at your feet. I'm not that girl." Now that was out of the way, she could move on to the task at hand.

"My lip is distracting?"

She rolled her eyes. "Don't pretend that you don't know what that looks like. It's kind of the equivalent of a girl flashing her boob. It's unexpected and sexy."

His laugh was low and full and moved through her like her vibrator when it had new batteries. Holy hell, this man was trouble. She needed to either stop drinking altogether or move another dozen feet from the heat of him.

"What time is your mother coming to town on Saturday?" Surely talk of his mother would cool things down.

"She'll get here around noon. Rather than dinner, I thought maybe we could have a late lunch. You don't really have to cook. We can take her to the diner."

"Oh." Was that disappointment threading through her? "I like to cook and don't get many opportunities. I don't mind making a late lunch." She'd been perusing recipes the last few days and thought she'd run a few by him on their "date" tonight.

"Okay, that sounds good. I don't want you to have to go through so much trouble. I know I suckered you into cooking when I propositioned you, but I'm flexible. What did you have in mind?"

"I was thinking of cooking garlic lime chicken over quinoa."

"Sold. I'll make sure we have white wine."

She stalled for a minute. "I'll pass on the wine, but if your mother likes wine, then I'd say buy her favorite. I'll stick with club soda that day."

He leaned back and looked at her in the same way she imagined he looked at perps. He was analyzing. It was apparent by his thoughtful but serious expression.

"There's a story there about wine I want to hear."

"Maybe another time. Right now, I need to know more about my sexy boyfriend, so I'm a believable girlfriend." *Did I really call him sexy?* He was, but feeding a man's ego was like feeding a tapeworm; they were never satisfied.

"You think I'm sexy?"

She waved him off. "This is pretend. Don't read more into this than it is."

His head nodded with a smoothness as if he'd just oiled his joints. "Right. Okay. What do you want to know?"

"I suppose I should know the basics like what you love and hate. Your favorite color and movie and song. Which side of the bed do you sleep on?

How many times you've been in love? Why those relationships didn't work out?"

"All that?"

"Do you want to be believable?"

"I don't think my mother will be that thorough."

She laid her hand on his. "Oh, love, you're her son. She's going to run me through the wringer. Just remember, no woman is ever going to be good enough for her boy."

"Not true," he said. "There's a lovely teacher she wants to hook me up with. One she's already vetted."

Deanna scooted her chair closer. "See, that means she'll be incredibly critical of your choice when she's already made one for you. I have to be at the top of my game." She clapped her hands and rubbed them together. There was one thing Deanna loved, and that was a challenge. "Shall we get started?"

CHAPTER SEVEN

Merrick answered her questions one by one. His favorite color ... blue. His favorite song was "Hotel California," but he loved anything from the Eagles. His favorite food was pizza. He preferred beer for casual affairs but loved an excellent cabernet with dinner. If his objective was to get drunk, whiskey would do it. He slept on the left side of the bed. Always put the cap back on the toothpaste and never left the toilet seat up.

"You're basically a perfect boyfriend?" She finished her beer and pushed the empty mug aside. "If that's the case, why are you single?"

"My career of choice is often relationship suicide." He signaled to Cannon to bring another round. "There's a lot of sharing a woman has to do when her boyfriend is in public service."

She snorted. "Maybe that's what we should call band members. Let's rename them public servants since they seem to serve much of the public."

"That wasn't the sharing I was referring to. Infidelity isn't really in my blood. If I'm in a relationship, I'm all in."

"Tell me about your first love?"

"I was nine, and she sat next to me in class. I brought her bags of Skittles, and she dumped me for a Snicker's gifting guy."

"Seriously? Snickers? The girl had no taste. Didn't she know that there's like ten percent fruit juice in Skittles? You were looking out for her best interests, and the other guy was giving her a sugar rush."

"There's no accounting for taste." He looked at Red, who was surrounded by women. Now that he was occupied with others, he seemed oblivious to Deanna's presence, making Merrick hate him all the more.

"Let's move forward. Who didn't want to share?"

He chuckled. "Most women don't want to share." As if she had eyes behind her head and could see the two girls on each side of Red, she said, "Some don't have an issue with it."

"What about you? Do you like to share?"

"Not really. I'm what you might call a greedy girl, but then again, I'm no spring chicken, and I've been wondering if maybe some of something is better than none of anything."

His emotions were almost always in check ... almost. But when a woman as beautiful as Deanna was willing to settle for less than what she deserved, it pissed him off. The problem was he didn't know if he was pissed at Deanna for thinking she deserved less or at Red for making her believe she wasn't worth his all.

"You shouldn't sell yourself short. You have a lot to offer."

Cannon brought the beers by and set them on the table. "Too bad this isn't the real deal because you two look good together." He pivoted on his heel and disappeared into the growing crowd.

"You think the whole town knows?" she asked.

"Nah, I think he knows because you talked to Sage."

She nodded. "Oh, right. Well, let's get back to you. Why do you think women don't want to share you with your career?"

"I'm a cop, so my job is never nine-to-five. Crime has no schedule."

"Or address," she said, obviously remembering their previous conversation.

"Then there's the whole danger aspect." He rubbed at his shoulder as if it hurt, even though it didn't. What smarted was that his last love left after the shooting. "My last girlfriend, Cassie, left me after I got grazed by a bullet. She couldn't handle knowing that each time I walked out the door, it might be my last."

Deanna brought her beer to her lips and took a sip. Her tongue darted out to swipe the foam from her upper lip before she set the mug down with a thunk. "Everyone leaves their house for what could be the last time each morning. A number of things can happen every day, from a lightning strike to a car accident. That's the silliest thing I've ever heard."

"You're a gem of a woman because you get that. While my job might inherently be more dangerous, even the safest job has risks."

"I'm more likely to kill someone than be killed. I mean ... I work with idiots." She flipped her hair over her shoulder and leaned forward. "Not Samantha. She's amazing, but the guys." She let out a breath that caught in her throat, causing the sexiest growl to escape. "Gray is probably the worst because he's been burned, and he won't go out of his way for anyone. He's nice enough but damaged. Then there was Alex." She giggled. It was a trill of a sound that rang like music in his ears. "I can't trust a man with longer and prettier hair than mine. Now that he's off the market, he's back in my good graces, but I'm waiting to see if the lovely locks grow again."

"What about Red?" He wanted to kick himself for asking, but the whole point of this experience was to make the man jealous, so Deanna could have what she wanted.

"He's ... he's Red. For the most part, he's a good guy who hides behind a bad-boy rock-star image, but deep down, I know he's not a bad man."

"Is this where you want to tell me about the wine?"

"Nope."

"Hey, I told you about the Skittles?"

She eyed him as if debating his trustworthiness. "Okay, but no judging." She gulped her beer. "Keep in mind that I've had a crush on Red for a very long time, but generally, it's never a good idea to mix work with relationships. So, here goes." She took a solid breath and began. "One day, he was in the studio laying down tracks. There was a bottle of wine, and I can drink a sailor under the table with hard liquor but give me a glass of wine, and I'm ... well ... let's just say we crossed the no fraternization line."

He smiled. "So, you're a cheap date."

She had quick reflexes and reached out to slug

his arm, hitting him square in the muscle. It wasn't hard enough to hurt, but powerful enough he could feel it.

"I can't believe you said that to me."

"Babe, you may be cheap, but I bet you're not easy."

"I'm pleading the fifth."

There was a tap on the mic, and Katie started karaoke night. Two hours and several beers later, the crowd had given up singing, and the dancing began. There wasn't a large space for moving bodies, but Merrick would have taken her for a twirl or two if this were a real date.

When something danceable came on, he stood and offered his hand. "Care to dance?"

"You want to dance with me?"

"You're my girl. I want to do everything with you." He led her to the dance floor and pulled her close. The rhythm was slow and sexy, which played into their well-executed plan. It didn't take but a minute for him to feel a tap on his shoulder, and when he turned, he found Red standing beside them, rocking to the beat. "Care if I jump in?"

Merrick could play it two ways. He could be a gentleman and step aside, or he could go with his gut. Usually, he thought with the head on his shoulders, but today he didn't want everything that was good to end with him giving Deanna over to that idiot. Technically speaking, he and Deanna had an agreement, and she was his "girlfriend" until Saturday dinner with his mother.

"Sorry, man. I don't share." He spun Deanna around and moved her farther away from Red.

"What are you doing?" she asked.

"What I said I would. I'm making him jealous. What he can't have, he'll want even more. Until Saturday, you're mine. Let him wallow in it for a while, okay?"

She seemed to ponder his request for a minute, then leaned her head on his chest and swayed to the beat. "Anything you want, love."

Wouldn't that be nice? There were a lot of things Merrick wanted. Right now, with Deanna in his arms and the music playing softly in the background, everything was almost perfect, almost because none of it was real.

CHAPTER EIGHT

Deanna paced the worn wooden floor in front of her living room window. She looked around and prayed everything was up to Merrick's mother's standards. She was a tidy person, and her home was warm and inviting. Or at least she thought so, but then again, it was her home, so she was partial. She hoped the flowers she set around the house drew eyes away from its imperfections like the peeling paint and missing baseboards. She'd even mowed the weeds, so they didn't have to trek through a forest to get to the door. Everything was a work in progress, and a woman smart and strong enough to raise Merrick single-handedly could appreciate the challenge.

She lifted her nose into the air and breathed in

the scent of garlic and cheese and the earthy aroma of quinoa. Just as she was about to check on dinner, his silver pickup pulled into her driveway, which sent her nerves jumping.

Sherman sat at her feet, wiggling his bottom and wagging his tail. "Traitor. Since when do you like my boyfriends?"

This isn't real, she reminded herself. Maybe she was nervous because she'd never cooked dinner for someone's mother, other than her own. That had to be it.

She stood behind the door and waited until they knocked, then pointed to Sherman's bed and told him to lie down. If a dog could scowl, Sherman just did, but he minded and slowly slogged his way to the corner cushion he called home.

She counted to ten, so she didn't seem too eager, and once the requisite wait was over, she smoothed her hair, put on a smile, and opened the door.

Excitement flooded through her at seeing Merrick. It was most likely the familiarity of having him nearby during a challenging situation. She'd come to depend on him in a short time.

"Welcome." A frog caught in her throat at the greeting, making it sound as if she croaked out the word. Clearing her throat, she giggled. "Come on in."

Merrick's mom stepped inside and pulled her

into a bear hug. "You can't even imagine how excited I am to meet you."

Deanna fell into the hug and stared at Merrick over his mother's shoulder.

He smiled and shrugged, then mouthed the words, "Thank you."

"I've heard lots of wonderful things about you and your daughter." Right then, she realized they hadn't ever talked about names. She had no idea what Merrick's mother's and sister's names were.

She stepped back and looked at the woman before her. She was tall but not a mountain like her son. There was a softness in her hazel eyes that told Deanna Merrick's mom was compassionate. But there was a firmness in her stance that said she didn't take any shit—from anyone.

"Can I get you a drink, Mrs. Buchanan?"

"Call me, Elsa." Elsa turned and took the bouquet from her son's hands. "These are for you."

Flowers from the Buchanans were becoming a thing she could get used to.

"Thank you, they're lovely." She stepped to the side. "Make yourselves comfortable, and I'll put these in water." She moved a few steps toward the kitchen. "How about a glass of wine? I've got a nice white chilled and ready to go."

Elsa walked toward the living room. Her fingers skimmed the fabric of the sofa as she moved around the room before taking the chair in the corner next to Sherman, who didn't budge.

"That sounds lovely." She looked down at Sherman, who inched over and laid his head across Elsa's shoe. "And who's this beautiful creature?"

"That's my fur baby, Sherman." She giggled. "He seems to like you. He certainly likes your son, which is saying a lot because my pup doesn't like anyone."

"Dogs and children are always good judges of character."

Like mother, like son.

"That's what I hear. I'll be right back." She looked at Merrick. "Merrick, love," she smiled. "Can you help me by pouring your mom a glass of wine?"

He rushed toward her. "Sure, babe, but how about a kiss first?"

Before she could say a word, he pressed his lips to hers. There was always a zing to his kisses like they were infused with caffeine or electricity.

"You two look cute together," Elsa commented.

Deanna stepped back, out of breath and flushed if the heat in her cheeks was any indicator. "Your son compliments me."

"He better, or I'll have to slap him upside the head." Elsa laughed.

"I meant that he makes me a better person."

"I know what you meant. I think it's cute, but don't be afraid to resort to a good cuffing if he pisses you off, and he will piss you off. He's a Buchanan, and that means he has a stubborn streak."

"I'll keep that in mind." She rushed to the kitchen and yanked out a vase from under the sink. While she cut the stems and arranged the flowers, Merrick poured the wine.

"Are you going to have a glass?"

She gave him an are-you-kidding-me look and shook her head. "I told you that wine is bad news for me. I'm a one and done girl."

He chuckled. "Right. I'll come over with a bottle once Mom leaves."

She reached out and cuffed him up the side of the head.

"Ouch."

"You deserved that. Now go deliver the wine."

He took one step before she dragged him back.

"Miss me already?" he asked in a low, sultry way.

"No, but I need information. You never told me your mom's or sister's name. I don't know the things I should," she whispered.

"Beth is my sister. Anything else?"

She leaned in. "Yes, stop kissing me. It muddles my brain."

"Muddles, huh?" He bent over and placed a quick kiss on her lips. "I think I like you muddled."

He spun around and walked away, leaving her questioning everything. Why did his kisses make her want more? That was so wrong when he wasn't the man she was after.

With the flower vase in her hands, she came back to the living room to find Elsa looking through her books.

"You're a lover of poetry?"

Poetry was one of her guilty pleasures, right up there with Hostess Cherry Pie.

"I'm a fan of many poets like JM Storm and Leo Christopher. One of my favorites these days is Rupi Kaur."

"She's quite a feminist in her writing, don't you think?"

Deanna set the flowers on the coffee table and sat next to Merrick on the sofa. "She's a strong woman who's experienced pain and joy and sorrow. I don't believe you can be creative without getting in touch with yourself. What draws me to her is the fact that she's a woman, and her words speak to the plight of all women."

Elsa returned to her chair. "I'm a huge fan as well. As women, we are more than a pretty face. Motherhood is a superpower, but not our only one. Tell me about your mother."

"My mother's name is Gretta, and she's my hero." She looked at Merrick before continuing. "Like you, my mom raised her children on her own."

"And your father?"

"He was in the military and did a tour of duty in Germany and never came back."

Elsa sipped her wine. "I'm sorry for your loss."

Deanna sat up. "Oh no, he's not dead. He just found someone else he liked better and stayed in Germany. He filed for divorce and never returned."

"Oh, well, then, I'm sorry for his loss."

"How was the drive, Mom?" Merrick wrapped his arm around Deanna and pulled her closer.

"It was lovely. The aspens are turning, so the fall colors lit up the forest." She breathed deeply as if she could smell the leaves. "What's cooking that smells so wonderful?"

"Garlic lime chicken over quinoa. It will be ready in about ten minutes."

"Perfect. That gives me time to find out more about how you met."

That was another thing they hadn't rehearsed.

"How we met?" She turned to Merrick. "Why don't you tell her our story, love." She saw him get a "deer in the headlight's" expression.

"How we met?" he repeated.

"Yes," Elsa said. "How did you meet? Was it

love at first sight?" She stared at the two of them sitting next to each other on the couch. "It's obvious you have a true love connection. I can't wait to hear your story."

"You read too many romance novels, Mom. Not everything is book-worthy."

Deanna saw a hint of disappointment flicker in Elsa's eyes. If the woman loved Nicholas Sparks, she was a romantic and had a soft spot for love stories. As Merrick's fake girlfriend, didn't she have a responsibility to provide her with a story to remember?

"Ours is book-worthy." She snuggled into his side for effect. "We met at the Corner Store. I work with difficult men." She cleared her throat. "I don't know if Merrick told you or not, but I'm the assistant to Samantha Black, who is the lead singer for Indigo."

"He did mention that you were in the entertainment field."

"Anyway, there's a lot of ego with musicians, and I was arguing with one of them. Merrick stepped in and became my hero, and he's been one ever since. You've raised a fine man, Mrs. Buchanan. You should be proud."

"He was an easy kid to raise. It doesn't surprise me he stepped in. He's always felt responsible for the people around him whether he knew them or not." She sipped her wine. "I'm sure that's why he went into law enforcement. Somehow, protect and serve runs through his veins."

The timer for the chicken dinged, and Deanna rose from the sofa. "Dinner is ready. Should we move to the table?"

Merrick stood and offered his hand to his mother. "Deanna is an excellent cook."

She wanted to bubble with laughter. All she'd ever fed him was a take-and-bake pizza.

"You're far too flattering for my good," she teased. "Don't get your mother's hopes up. We could be rushing her to Doc's for a stomach pumping in a few minutes."

They made their way to the table and took seats.

Deanna plated up her chicken and accessorized the meal with a parsley sprig while Merrick poured more wine.

"You're not drinking?" Elsa asked when Deanna's glass remained empty.

"I'm not much of a drinker." She reached for the bottle of sparkling water and filled her glass. "Wine goes straight to my head."

Elsa picked up her wineglass and held it out in front of her. "I'd like to propose a toast."

Deanna and Merrick picked up their glasses and waited.

"To moderation in all things, except in love. May you find your hearts entwined forever and your bodies long enough to give me a grandchild."

"Mom," Merrick said with a hint of warning.

"What? There's nothing wrong with planting a seed."

He shook his head. "Are we talking about you or me?"

His mother smiled. "I'd prefer you to plant the seed, and I'll watch it grow."

A warm feeling fluttered in Deanna's belly. It was that same feeling she got when she drank wine —a drunk feeling, but this time caused by words and not alcohol.

CHAPTER NINE

"I don't know, Mom, Deanna has a busy schedule." Merrick poured a cup of coffee and inhaled the rich scent of freshly ground beans. "She's got a lot of people to manage." Was her schedule busy? He couldn't say. They never discussed her job or the kind of pressure it put her under.

"I like her, Merrick. She's the perfect mix of sweet and sassy, and she doesn't seem to put up with your shit."

Mom certainly homed in on the "I cooked so you clean" statement after Saturday's meal.

"I like her too. It's why I chose her ... or she chose me." That part was getting muddy. She made the first move, but he persuaded her to help him fool his mom. They were complicit in the plan that unfolded so beautifully. This was a problem because he didn't count on his mother wanting to see them again so soon. After last night's success, it would be hard to fake a quick breakup. They pulled the dinner date off so well, even he believed it was real.

That kiss good night was real, even if it wasn't. Red was an effing idiot for letting a woman who could kiss like Deanna get away.

"I'm not taking no for an answer. If you don't say yes, I'll call her myself."

Mom was not a pushover, and she'd press until he caved.

"I'll ask her." He couldn't let his mom get in the middle of the situation, or she'd have Deanna in Denver picking out wedding dresses and a cake.

"Perfect, call me tonight. I'll make your favorite meal."

"Burger King Whoppers?" he teased.

"If my arms were long enough, I'd reach all the way to Aspen Cove and slap you upside the head."

"I'll ask her. Now let me get to work and stop bugging me."

"I only pester because I care."

"Bye, Mom." He made a kissing sound into the phone and hung up.

Now what was he supposed to do? There was no plan to continue the ruse beyond Saturday. He poured his cup of coffee into an insulated mug and walked out the door. Women were trouble. It started with mothers and bled all the way down to sweet, pretty pop star assistants whose kisses were addictive.

He hopped inside his truck and drove to Main Street, parking behind the sheriff's station. In the alleyway was Cannon and Bowie accepting delivery for the bait and tackle store.

"You need some help?"

Cannon nodded toward the stack of boxes, piled four high at the back door. "We never turn down free labor."

Merrick hurried to assist. "What's the big delivery? I thought the season was almost over."

Bowie nodded. "It is, but this angler's club decided to do a fishing tournament on the lake. The one thing I know about anglers is they'll want the latest and greatest. They are a competitive bunch and will spend whatever it takes to catch the biggest fish and win the prize." He hefted a box and led them inside the shop.

At the counter, Bowie tore into the box and pulled out several reels and poles.

"Those look mighty fancy for trout," Merrick said.

"Personally, I'd take the thirty-dollar Kastking Centron over this Penn, but that's because I'm frugal. You know how people can be; they aren't happy with what they have and need to have the next best thing," Bowie said.

"I know all too well how people dump perfectly good equipment for something shinier and prettier." That attitude wasn't exclusive to fishing equipment. It happened with people too.

"It's a shame," Bowie added. "Shiny and pretty isn't always the best bet."

"All a matter of taste, I suppose."

Cannon came inside carrying another box. "What are you two going on about?"

Merrick shrugged. "Just how shallow people can be." He picked up an old rod sitting on the counter. "Why would anyone discard this when it's perfectly good?" He pressed the spool release, and the weight hit the ground.

"Hey." Bowie took it from his hand. "That's my reel, and no one is getting rid of her."

"Her?" Merrick asked.

"A good reel is like a good woman. When you find the perfect one, you treat her right. You baby her and make sure she's got what she needs." He held up the reel. "This needed a tune-up. I cleaned her and replaced her line. If you don't take care of the things important to you, they break down."

"Are we talking about reels or women?"

Cannon tore open another box and pulled out bait and flies.

"I'd say we're talking about both. If you don't treat your woman right, she'll go looking for another man. If you don't take care of your fishing pole, she won't be of any use to you either."

"Speaking of other men ... how did the 'date' with Deanna go?" Cannon asked.

Merrick rubbed his chin. "We accomplished what we set out to do."

Bowie shook his head. "That's a woman who's using the wrong kind of bait to catch what she's after." Bowie moved to the lures that Cannon stacked on the counter. "Take this shit." He held up the PowerBait. The neon yellow jar sparkled in his hand. "You'll catch the fish, but what's the fun in getting something so easy? In my experience, easy has never been satisfying."

"She wants what she wants."

Cannon grunted. "She only wants what she thought she had. I mean, carp looks pretty, but once you've had a taste, you know to throw it back. Maybe what Deanna needs is to taste a bass. Now those are worth keeping. Maybe you're her bass."

"Are we seriously having a conversation about fish and women?"

Bowie laughed. "As silly as it sounds, it makes sense. My Katie is a bass, and she's a keeper."

Cannon snorted. "I'd say Sage is more of a cat-fish these days. She's prickly, and it hurts when you're her intended victim. Then again, she's pregnant, and carrying my kid can't be easy."

"Lucky bastards," Merrick said.

"You can be lucky too." Bowie tossed Merrick a container of worms. "Use the right bait, and you'll get the perfect fish."

He chuckled. "I'm not looking to reel anything in at this time. In my experience, law enforcement and women are a bad mix."

"Only if she's got a bench warrant out on her." Cannon turned and walked toward the door. "Got to go. I've got my delivery coming in about twenty minutes." He put his finger to his lips. "I ordered this fancy thing called a Snoo Smart Sleeper. It's supposed to help the baby sleep longer. I figured if it doesn't work for the baby, I'll stick Sage in it. My woman needs her rest."

"You're an idiot," Bowie said. "Those things cost too much."

Cannon raised his hands. "Happy wife—happy life."

"I should go too. I'm sure there's paperwork to fill out. No doubt, Mrs. Brown's cat caused some havoc over the weekend."

Bowie followed him out the back door. "What's it like turning in car chases for cats in costume?"

"It's heaven."

"You know what heaven is?" He pointed down the alley to the bakery. "It's waking up to your best friend and looking in her eyes and knowing that your life would never be the same without her."

"I'll let you know if I find her."

"Maybe you already have, but you're too worried some other angler has a better chance at reeling her in. All you can do is toss out your line and give it a shot. Either she bites, or she doesn't. If she doesn't, she wasn't the fish for you."

Did they just compare women to fish again and the chase to bait and a fishing line? If his mother were there, she would have cuffed them all upside the head.

He walked inside the station and found Poppy filing paperwork. He picked up the keys for the cruiser. "I'm making the rounds. Is there anything I need to be aware of?"

She shook her head. "Tom is missing. There's a BOLO for a cat in a Superman costume. He shouldn't be hard to find. I'd keep my eyes to the sky. If I were Tom, I'd hide in the highest tree."

He shook his head. "If I were him I'd jump to my death and hope the cape didn't work. Poor cat."

Outside, he was about to hop in the cruiser and take off when he saw Deanna enter the diner. Thoughts of Mom ran through his head, followed by Bowie and Cannon's fishing analogies. Maybe it was time to toss his line into the water—at least long enough to snag another fake date. Was that what he wanted? How long could he keep up the game they were playing?

Red showed his jealousy on Wednesday night, but Deanna said nothing of where that went. Were they already back together?

A slow burn fired in his belly. She deserved better than an egotistical musician with a line of groupies waiting to take their turn. A man like Red could never appreciate a single daisy in a bouquet of roses—never see the beauty in the simple flower. Deanna was a daisy who happened to live on a street by the same name. Was that an accident or the universe recognizing the truth?

She was beautiful and resilient, pretty, and strong. She seemed to grow wherever she was planted and thrived in whatever conditions the world threw at her. Deanna was different from most women. She was undoubtedly different from Cassie, and she understood life and its risks. *Everyone leaves their house for what could be the last time each morning*, she'd said, and she was right. With that in the forefront of his mind, he walked into the diner, ready to seize the day because life was uncertain.

He glanced around looking for her and found

her tucked into the front corner booth by the window. Before her was a stack of papers an inch thick.

"Hey, beautiful." He slid into the booth seat across from her. "Did you miss me?" If she said yes, what would he do? Kiss her again? A tingle raced up his body to his lips. He'd like that.

"Hey, you?" She straightened the pile and shoved it aside. "You want coffee?"

It wasn't the confirmation he was hoping for, but she pushed aside her work to focus on him, and that felt good. How many people only gave a fraction of their attention to the ones they loved? This woman gave him her undivided attention, and she had no interest in loving him. That said something about her character.

"Are you asking me on a date?"

A blush rose from her neckline to her cheeks. "No, I'm buying you coffee."

It was only an inch or two, but his heart sank. "That's a start."

Maisey walked over with her loafers squeaking and the pot of coffee swinging in her hand. "You two want a cup of coffee?"

Merrick turned over the two mugs on the table. "Fill 'er up." He grabbed the sugar and measured two teaspoonfuls into Deanna's cup. It's what she added to her coffee Saturday night when they ate cake and enjoyed a cup just before Mom left. "She'll need cream."

Deanna stared at him but said nothing.

"Are you hungry, Sweetheart?" His eyes left her and turned to Maisey. "I'd love a plate of cakes and a side of bacon, and I'll take the check today."

"Wait ... what?" Deanna shook her head hard enough to send her ponytail wagging. "This date is my treat."

His lips twitched before lifting into a grin. "So, it is a date?"

She opened and closed her mouth several times, and when nothing came out, he held up two fingers. "Bring Deanna the same. She's so hungry she's left speechless."

"Oh, honey, she's hungry all right, but looking at you two, I'd say her lack of words has nothing to do with her desire for food." Maisey pivoted and walked away.

"Oh my God, did she just accuse me of being hungry for you?"

He chuckled. "Maybe. Are you?"

Her hand came out and clipped his shoulder. How she got it across the table so fast he couldn't fathom. "What's wrong with you?" She looked around and leaned into the center of the table. "Our deal is done, and there's no reason for you to pretend to be my boyfriend anymore," she whispered.

"Did it work? Do you have Red back?" He leaned against the booth back and watched her with his interrogator's eye.

"It's too soon to tell. We haven't seen each other since Wednesday night." The light in her eyes died at the mention of nearly five days ago. "I'll see him at work today. We have to go over album cover designs and the playlist order."

Men were simple creatures. Deep down, they were knuckle draggers, and when it came to women, their base instincts took over. If Red wanted Deanna, he would be a chest-pounding, club-bearing asshole until he got what he wanted.

"You'll have to let me know how that goes."

He already knew how it would go. Deanna would arrive at work hopeful and leave feeling dejected. The only reason Red acted as if he cared on Wednesday was that he didn't want to be ignored.

"How's your mom?"

"She's good." He sipped his coffee. "Speaking of my mom. I have a proposition for you."

CHAPTER TEN

Did he say proposition? She cocked her head and smiled. "Do I have to cook again?"

"You didn't have to the last time." He looked down at his coffee before raising his eyes to meet hers. "I offered to bring you both here."

What was that she saw in his face? Regret? Remorse? Hope? "I know. I didn't mind cooking for your mother. She was remarkably easy to please."

"It's because she liked you." He folded his napkin in half and then in half again before unfolding and pressing it flat with his palm. "Maybe if you weren't so likable, I wouldn't be in this position."

"What position is that?"

"I need another fake date."

Why did the thought of one more date with Merrick send her nerves aflutter?

"You what?"

"I'm asking you to come with me on a date. Only this time, it's in Denver at my mother's house."

"Here you go," Maisey said as she dropped off the plates of pancakes and bacon. From her front pocket, she pulled a container of maple syrup. "You kids need anything else?"

"Sanity?" Deanna said.

"If we sell it, I'm sold out. Besides, nothing wrong with a little crazy in your life. Sane is equivalent to boring. Live on the edge. It's more exciting."

"Yeah," Merrick said, staring at Deanna. "Live on the edge."

Maisey was gone, and Deanna took in Merrick. There was that look of hope again on his face, it was a lift of his brow and a slight quirk of his mouth. Mostly it showed up in his rich, coffee-colored eyes. If eyes could beg, his were on their knees.

"This is insane. You're my fake boyfriend, and I've had better dates with you than the man I'm trying to attract. Hell, I've had more dates with you." *Why did I just tell him that? I mean, it is true, but that doesn't mean anything, does it?*

"We've only had one."

She lifted her eyes and shook her head. "Exactly. What happened with Red wasn't even a date. It was ..."

He picked up a piece of bacon. "What was it?" He took a bite and chewed.

"I thought it was the beginning of something."

"If that was the beginning, Red has a slow starter."

"What the hell am I doing?"

Merrick slathered his pancakes in butter and put a healthy pour of thick maple syrup on top. She watched it ooze from the middle to drip down the sides. That was how she was feeling right now, like syrup, with no direction but down.

"You're coming to Denver with me on Thursday for dinner."

With a piece of bacon in her hand, she nibbled the end and considered the offer. It wasn't like she had a lot of weeknight options. Aspen Cove wasn't the hot spot for singles on a Thursday night. Outside of flying into the Denver International Airport when she came here to purchase Samantha's house, she hadn't spent much time in the mile-high city.

"What about Sherman?"

He frowned. "Are you going to use the dog as your excuse?"

She nodded. "Yes, and it's not an excuse. He's not used to being left alone. There's no doggie day camp in town."

"You can bring him."

"You can't say that. You haven't even asked your mother."

He chuckled. "I don't have to, but if it makes you feel better ..." He pulled his phone from his pocket and sent a text.

A moment later, his phone chimed with an incoming message, and he turned it to show her.

Tell her to bring Sherman. I can't wait to see you both.

Love, Mom

"What do you say?" he asked.

She didn't have a reason to say no and every reason to say yes. Merrick was a nice guy, and he'd done his part to help her. And yes, she'd done her part to help him, but somehow it seemed weighted to his side because spending time with his mother wasn't a hardship. If the truth is told, she rather enjoyed the day she cooked for them.

Thoughts of their first date brought memories of his kisses. Kisses that could turn a caterpillar into a butterfly. Something about his lips charged her body and soul and made her want to sprout wings and fly.

"Can we stop at Krispy Kreme on the way back?"

"That's your price for pretending to be my girlfriend?" He shook his head. "You have to value yourself more."

She forked a bite of pancakes. "That's just the beginning of what it's going to cost you. I might need a Costco run too."

His mouth dropped open in mock shock. "Not Costco ... anything but Costco."

"And Trader Joes for some Two Buck Chuck."

He rubbed his beard. She'd never been a fan of facial hair, but on Merrick, it fit. When he kissed her, she expected it to be rough and scruffy, but it was soft, and he smelled good.

"How do they get away with that? It's 2.99, so really, it's Three Buck Chuck."

"Even at three dollars a bottle, it's still a bargain."

"Funny for the girl who doesn't drink wine."

Damn cop in him caught everything. "Oh, I drink it but not with men I'd like to ... not in mixed company."

He tried to suppress a smile but failed. "So ... is that a yes?"

To prolong his agony, she took a few more bites of pancake and sips of coffee before she offered him a handshake to seal the deal.

"It's a deal."

"You aren't a great negotiator. You could have roped me in for far more."

She pushed her plate away and patted her belly. "You could have gotten me to say yes for far less."

"I still think you don't value yourself enough."

"So, you've said." She looked at her silverware and lined them up from tallest to smallest. "But then again, you don't know all that much about me."

He pulled out his wallet and tossed twenty dollars on the table. Maisey's was cheap, so that twenty left her almost a ten-dollar tip.

Deanna liked that Merrick saw the value of people and their service.

"Let's remedy that. We've got a three-hour drive to Denver, and I want to know everything about you."

"I'm not all that exciting to take up three hours."

"Again, you sell yourself short."

She narrowed her eyes. "I already said yes, you don't need to flatter me."

He leaned back into the booth. "I'm not accustomed to blowing smoke up anyone's ass. What you see is what you get."

"Unless it's your mother, right?"

He exhaled a breath with the force of a storm. "I'm not proud of myself for the deceit." He breathed in deeply and released a sigh. "I'll come clean, but what I need now is time to adjust here in Aspen Cove without her meddling in my love life.

When I'm ready to settle down, it will be with a woman I choose."

"You're lucky she loves you enough to care."

He nodded. "You're right, but I'm not sixteen, and I don't need dating advice. Besides, generally speaking, she's not a fan of who I choose."

"Meaning, she didn't like Cassie."

"Didn't like is putting it lightly. I'm pretty sure if Cassie was on fire and Mom was standing next to a bucket of water, she would have knocked it over and walked away."

Deanna let out a giggle that turned into a full laugh that ended with a snort. "I can see your mom doing that. She doesn't seem to be one to put up with anyone's crap." She drank the final gulp of coffee and set her mug on the table with a thump. "Was she wrong about Cassie?"

"No. She was right. Cassie was egocentric. I mean, she loved the Policeman's Ball but hated the long hours. She enjoyed the perks of me knowing people when she got a ticket, but she hated the late-night calls. She loved the paycheck more than she loved me."

Deanna lifted her shoulder. "Sometimes that saying, 'mother knows best' is true."

"Meddling mothers are as dangerous as a hurricane."

"I bet your mother is a Cat 5 when she's angry."

He chuckled. "There isn't a category for my mother when she's angry."

Deanna rose from the booth. "Then let's not make her angry, love." She bent over and kissed his cheek. "I have to go to work, but I'll see you Thursday." She took a step away. "Thanks for breakfast."

"Anything for you, babe."

She breathed in his kindness. "Why can't you be real?"

CHAPTER ELEVEN

Merrick watched her exit her house with Sherman tucked under her arm. She got halfway down the walkway before she turned and headed back to the front door to recheck the lock. After two pulls on the handle, she spun around and moved toward him again.

Today she walked with confidence. He found that appealing, or maybe it was the sway of her hips he paid attention to. Both coming and going, Deanna was an attractive woman. What made her doubly so was her quick wit and easygoing nature. *I need to stop thinking about how perfect she is and start remembering this is an act.*

He jumped out of the truck and rushed around to open her door. "I put a blanket in the back seat for Sherman, but if you think he'll be more comfortable in the front, I can move it." He sounded like a high school boy trying to win over his first date. Bringing Deanna home to his mom made it seem real. *But it isn't real, this is just pretend.*

"He's fine back there. The blanket is a nice touch. I'm sure he appreciates it."

He opened the King Cab door, and she placed Sherman on the blanket. The dog looked at it skeptically before plopping in the middle and looking at them with an expression that said, *home James.*

"Does he travel well, or will we need to stop often?"

She giggled. "He's been more places than the average human. I've carted him on planes and cruise ships. I even tucked him in a backpack and took him hiking in the Andes. He wasn't a fan of that trip." She took her place in the front seat and pulled a bag of kibble from her purse. "I normally bring a doggy bag, but he associates that with the hike and hides. I guess it's kind of like PTSD for pets."

He stood at her open door and took in the domestic scene. If he let his mind wander, he could imagine being with her and Sherman being their pet. If he allowed his mind to reach further, he could even see a couple of kids sitting in the King Cab.

He shook his head and closed the door. As he rounded the pickup, he reminded himself what this was, a mutual agreement.

Once inside, he started the engine. As he pulled out of her driveway, a fancy sports car edged in front of the house, and Red got out.

"Just wave goodbye," Merrick said.

He slowed down to a crawl so the asshole could get a good glimpse of the one who got away and the man who was driving her in a different direction. Right then, he knew this was going very differently than planned.

"Should I open my window and say something?" She glanced at Merrick. "He's standing there with his mouth hanging open."

Merrick stopped the truck and opened the passenger window with the push of a button. "Hey, Red," he said. "Did you need something?"

Red's mouth snapped shut, and he stood there for a moment. "I wanted to talk to Deanna."

"Sorry, man. We're on our way to dinner with my mother." He reached over and took her hand. "You ready, babe?" He held her hand firmly in his. "She'll be back to work on Monday. Can it wait until then?"

Red's face changed colors. "This isn't about wor—."

Merrick raised the window and backed out of the driveway.

"Oh my God, what the hell was that about?" Deanna asked.

"That was the look of a man who knows he made a mistake, and right now, he's trying to figure out how to rectify the situation."

They turned from Daisy to Main Street and headed south toward Denver.

"What if he only wants me because he can't have me?"

Merrick had let her hand go to drive, but he covered it again with his. He loved how it fit entirely in his palm. "At least he's thinking about things, and that's good, right?"

"I guess, but I'd rather he was pursuing me because he liked me, not because he's playing tug of war with another dog, and I'm the rope."

"If that were the case, I'd win. I'm a Rottweiler when it comes to what's mine. I'm fiercely loyal and protective. If this were an actual game, he'd never win. I'm a formidable opponent."

She turned her head and stared out the side window. "I'll never understand men."

He squeezed her hand before letting it go and placing it back on the steering wheel.

"We're simple. That's the problem. Most women think we're more complicated than we appear to be. Not so. We've barely evolved past our Neanderthal ancestors."

"Where do you keep your club?"

A laugh that started deep in his gut bubbled up and burst forth. "You want to talk about my club?" His club was tucked inside his jeans. Just the mention of it gave it a rise. He silently talked it down.

A glance at Deanna told him the comment left her on the heated side, too, if the red in her cheeks was any indication.

"Yep," she said. "You're all alike. It would serve me well not to romanticize. Men survive off of basic instinct. All they need is sex and food. I've found that for most, clothing is optional."

"Don't forget a big-screen TV and Sunday football."

"And beer," she added.

"More of a wine guy myself."

"That reminds me." She stuck her hand back in her bag and pulled out a bottle of wine. "I brought this. I was also taught never to come empty-handed."

"What else is in that purse?" It wasn't a huge bag, but it held a lot. "Dead body? Weapon?"

"It holds a lot despite its size." She turned the label so he could see it.

He glanced at the bottle. "19 Crimes?"

"I thought it was funny, and the guy at the

liquor store said it was good." She twisted in her seat to face him. "There's also an app, and if you point your phone's camera at the bottle, the character on the front will animate and tell you his story." She tucked the bottle back into her bag. "I thought your mom might find it entertaining."

"Speaking of Mom. We should probably shore up our story. How about you start? Where were you born?"

"San Francisco, but I was raised in Los Angeles. I went to school at UCLA and got my degree in entertainment management."

"How long have you worked for Samantha?"

She touched her chin and tapped her fingers several times as if she were calculating the years. "I was with her when she started. I was a new graduate, and I was cheap. She was the new kid on the block and broke, so it was a match made in heaven. She's my longest relationship. We've been together for about eight years. What about you? Why a cop?"

He rocked his head from side to side. There were a lot of reasons he became a cop. His mother thought it was because he was born to serve and protect, and that might have some truth to it. Mostly, he wanted to make sure the good people stayed good, and the bad people remained behind bars. There was one event that changed the trajectory of his life.

"When I was about fourteen, I witnessed something that changed everything. We lived in downtown Denver. Not a bad area, but there were a lot of transients. Mom worked at the public library, and I used to pick my sister up at school and bring her there where we'd do our homework and wait for my mom to get off work."

When he blinked, he could almost see the day unfold as if it were happening again.

"One day, when I got there, Mom was at the door guiding people outside. Her face was ashen and panic-stricken. Worse so when she saw we had arrived. She kept pacing the steps and yelling, 'Where are they?'"

"What happened?"

"Turns out, a homeless man, or maybe a hopeless man, locked himself in one of the study rooms and was threatening to commit suicide. Mom had called the police twenty minutes before, but they hadn't shown up. She told me to take my sister home, but I only walked far enough to get out of her sight. From behind a tree, I watched it all unfold. The police showed up about five minutes later. They went inside, but it was too late. At the time, the Denver force was understaffed, or that's what they told Mom, but

I wasn't sure that was the case. Maybe a homeless man wasn't as important to them. I always wondered if they'd gotten there quicker, could they have saved him? Right then, I knew I wanted to help people."

"But you moved."

That was always something that pricked his conscience. "I did. Sometimes you have to serve yourself to serve others. As the years went by, I did my best to help my community, but that close call was a wake up for me. There are a lot of ways to serve and protect. Ways I don't need to be in the line of fire to do."

This time, it was her hand that reached forward to grab his. She pulled it to her lips and kissed his knuckles before dropping her hand to the bench but not letting go. And for the next hour, she held on to him.

The drive from Aspen Cove to Aurora, a suburb of Denver, went by quickly, and he was disappointed their time alone was over.

By the time they arrived at his mother's, he knew her favorite flower and candy. Knew that she wasn't a fan of olives but loved tomatoes. Her favorite fruit was a peach, but the ones with white flesh because they were sweeter. She liked chocolate but preferred milk to dark. She loved to dress up and go out but didn't have much occasion to do so. There was a fabulous pair of heels in her closet that had been waiting for a date.

"Are you ready for this?" He pulled into the driveway and killed the engine.

"Actually, I am. I like your mother. Not only is she funny, but she's engaging and kind. Besides, I bet I could talk her into showing me some embarrassing pictures of you."

"She probably has the photo albums on the coffee table waiting for you."

"Are *you* ready for this?"

In truth, he was. Somehow he lucked out. If he had to be in a relationship with anyone, fake or real, Deanna was a good choice.

"Let's go, and make Mom swoon, babe."

She unbuckled her seat belt. "I'm all yours, love."

He exited the truck and worked his way around to open her door. *Too bad that isn't true.*

With Sherman in Deanna's arms and his hand at the small of her back, he guided her toward the front door.

It burst open, and out came his sister, Beth.

"Hey, you." She flung herself into him like she was sacking him on the football field. "I've missed you."

He stumbled back. "I'll be feeling that greeting tomorrow. What are you doing here?"

Beth smiled and looked at Deanna. "If my big brother is in love, I'm totally going to be around to witness it." She stepped sideways and faced Deanna. "I already like you better than the last one. She had that resting bitch face down to a science. You ... you look nice."

Deanna lifted a brow, and he was confident the shake in her shoulders was her attempt to hold back a laugh.

"Thanks ... I think."

Beth leaned in and ruffled Sherman's fur. "And you like animals. That's a plus for me because I have several. I'm a regular Dr. Doolittle."

"Beth is a vet tech at the shelter. She's also a sucker for sad eyes."

"Someone has to love the ugly ones." She gave Deanna an exaggerated wink. "But, you already know that if you've fallen for my brother." Without asking, she reached for Sherman, who happily climbed into Beth's arms. "Are you ready to face the gauntlet?"

"What do you mean? Who else is in there?"

"Just Mom and some lady named Sandra. I don't think Mom was expecting her, but you know how Mom is, she'd never ask her to leave, so it's five for dinner."

"This won't be good."

Deanna cocked her head. "Who's Sandra?"

"She's the woman Mom was setting me up with before she found out about you."

Beth laughed. "Oh, this is going to be so much fun."

"Yep," Deanna said. "I'm all about the fun." As they started for the door, Deanna leaned in closer and said, "You're going to owe me big for this one, love."

CHAPTER TWELVE

The air smelled of sage and brown gravy. Deanna closed her eyes briefly and let the scent take her back home to her mother's Thanksgiving table, which would be covered in savory dishes from turkey to stuffing to the same sage gravy she smelled in Elsa Buchanan's house.

"Did your mom make a turkey?"

Merrick wrapped his arm around her shoulders like it belonged there, and in truth, it felt comfortable. As if her shoulders were made for his strong arm to rest on.

"It's my favorite. Why do we have to only have it once a year?"

Deanna turned to face him, causing his arm to slide from her. "Why didn't you tell me?" She lifted her bag. "I brought red wine when I should have brought white."

She balled her fist and was ready to tap him with it when his mother walked in.

"You two fighting?" His mom had a way of raising her brows that opened her eyes wider and somehow made it seem like she could look into a person's soul. Deanna only hoped that she didn't see the truth.

Merrick placed a quick peck on Deanna's lips and turned to face his mother. "I'm in trouble because I didn't tell Deanna we were having turkey, and she brought you a bottle of red wine."

His mother waved them off. "It's wine ... we don't follow silly rules here. Who cares about the color of the meat? It's a crazy rule, no doubt made by some cook that liked things matchy matchy." She walked over and pulled her in for a hug. "Good to see you again."

Deanna gave Merrick the side-eye before smiling at his mother. "You too. I was more than excited to visit today."

"Come into the kitchen. It's where all the fun begins. Besides, I have some appetizers like bacon-wrapped dates. And although pork is considered the other white meat, I think it will pair beautifully with a glass of red." His mom led them into the kitchen where Beth sat next to a pretty blonde.

Elsa grabbed several glasses and came to the table while she and Merrick took a seat.

"Forgive me." Elsa did a flourish with her hand, a kind of game show host unveiling, and said, "This is Sandra; she works where I work."

Sandra leaned over the table and offered her hand to Deanna first and then to Merrick. She barely glanced at Deanna, but her eyes were all over Merrick. She had the look of a spider ready to eat a fly—Merrick was the fly.

A thread of jealousy twisted around Deanna's spine. It pulled and tugged at feelings she had no right to feel. Jealousy? Over what?

"Nice to meet you," Deanna squeaked out. Her voice always had that *mouse caught in a trap* sound when she wasn't completely honest.

Merrick looked at her and smiled as if he knew she was lying. Knew what she was feeling inside. Maybe it was his laser-focused cop instincts.

"Hey, babe, do you want wine or something else?"

He was baiting her. She couldn't drink wine, or the whole day would go to hell.

"Something else, please."

"You don't like wine but brought a bottle?" Sandra asked.

Deanna opened her mouth to speak, but Merrick got the words out first. "Deanna loves wine.

She has excellent taste too. The tannins often affect her head, so she goes lightly with the grape juice."

"Migraines?" Sandra asked. "I get that too, but mostly with reds."

"Here we go." Elsa was back with a tray of wine glasses filled with white wine and one with club soda. She handed Deanna hers first. "If I recall, you prefer the bubbly, non-alcoholic, and a slice of lime. I thought we'd start with the white and drink your lovely bottle of red later."

"You are so thoughtful." Speaking of thoughtful, she reached for her bag, which she'd hung from the back of the chair, and took out the bottle of wine. "This is it. Not only do I hear the wine is amazing, but it's interactive. It's got this thing called a living wine label. Have you seen it before?"

She looked around to see their faces, and all four, Elsa, Sandra, Beth, and Merrick, stared at her like she was speaking in tongues.

"Seriously, seeing is believing. Look at it." She pulled her phone out and positioned the bottle so they could see it and her screen at the same time. When the label came to life, everyone gasped. It told the story of a man accused of treason and sent from England to Australia, which was then a penal colony.

"Fascinating," Elsa said.

"Nifty party trick," Beth added. She hadn't let

go of Sherman since they entered the house. "Will he be okay if I let him down?"

"Yep, but he'll need to go outside soon."

Beth got up. "I'll take him now."

Beth left, and when Deanna looked at Sandra, she appeared bored.

"So, how long have you been going out?" Sandra lifted her shoulders. "I only ask because only a week or so ago, I was supposed to be going on a date with Merrick."

Merrick, who'd just taken a sip of his wine, nearly spit it across the table.

Deanna picked a napkin up from the center and handed it to him. "It's been a whirlwind of a romance. I'm sorry you missed out. We met when he first came to Aspen Cove." She turned to look at him and took him in from the top of his head to the toe of his fancy loafers. The kind that looked like they were hand-rubbed and made in Italy. "A man like Merrick is hard to miss and impossible to ignore."

"You're right." Sandra sighed, but her eyes didn't leave Merrick.

"Hey," he said. "I'm right here, so talk to me. Besides, I'm not a side of beef."

Beth walked inside with Sherman at her heels. She was laughing and obviously heard the exchange. "Oh, look who doesn't appreciate being objectified. Welcome to our world. It's okay for a man to undress a woman with his eyes but not the other way?"

"I'm off the market, so the only one doing the undressing these days is Deanna." He turned and winked at her.

That one flirtatious act made her stomach tumble, and her ovaries dance.

Oh my God, what is wrong with me? Why am I acting like that actually meant something?

"At least someone is getting undressed," Elsa mumbled.

Deanna snorted at the boldness of the Buchanan family. It was like being home with her mother and sisters where nothing was taboo, and everything was talked about as if ordinary.

"Taste one of those dates." Elsa didn't wait for her to reach for one but grabbed a toothpick and speared one, lifting it to her mouth. She opened obediently and took the small bite. First, she was hit with the salt of the bacon and then the sweetness of the date. As a surprise, there was the crunch of a nut inside.

"Oh my God, that's so good. I need the recipe."

"It's a family secret," Beth piped in.

"What's so secret about shoving a nut up a date's ass and wrapping it in bacon?" Sandra asked.

"There's more to it than that," Elsa answered.

She picked up another date and handed it to Deanna. "I'll make sure you go home with it. Merrick loves them." She glanced around the small kitchen table. "Shall we move into the dining room where we'll have more room?"

They all took seats around the dining room table. Sherman curled into a ball in the corner, just hoping for someone to drop a morsel.

Elsa served a dinner that was a regular holiday feast, including all the fixin's.

Though every meal required one annoying relative, they had Sandra, who continued to flirt with Merrick as if she had a chance to steal her man. *Her man.* Somehow, during the evening, she'd come to think in terms of possession, and until they were back in Aspen Cove, he was hers, at least by agreement.

She had to hand it to him. He doted on her like a loving boyfriend, and some part of him was always touching her. She once had a yellow lab that was the same. It didn't matter where she was, her dog had to touch her somehow. Merrick was proving as loyal as her once-beloved pet.

They took a seat in the living room where Elsa set out trays of treats like cookies and brownies.

"Next time, I'll have to bring you these turtle brownies from B's Bakery. My friend Katie makes them." She was talking about next time like it was a given.

"I'd love that. There's nothing like a good brownie."

"I make a good brownie even though I'm not a fan of chocolate," Sandra said.

Beth frowned. "It's a good thing it didn't work out with you and my brother then because he's a huge fan of chocolate and bacon-wrapped dates, and it would appear Deanna." She smiled sweetly, but there was a fire in her eyes that said she'd been picking up the slights and barbs all night.

Elsa cleared her throat. "I imagine you'll need to get going since you have class tomorrow." All eyes went to Sandra.

"Right." She jumped up from the couch like she'd been yanked to her feet, which she sort of was with the not-so-subtle dismissal. "Thanks for inviting me to stay." She turned to Deanna. "Nice meeting you." She looked at Merrick. "Always a day late and a dollar short." She grabbed her bag and headed for the door.

Beth disappeared for a moment and came back with the bottle of 19 Crimes and Sherman. "She's lucky I didn't hit her over the head with this, or they'd have to rename the brand 20 Crimes, and you'd all be visiting me in prison." She popped the cork. "After that dinner, we all need a glass of wine." She poured everyone a glass, including Deanna, and waited for Elsa to return.

"Oh, Lord. I'm so sorry. She's far nicer at work. I just don't know what to say."

"You can say you'll stop matchmaking," Merrick said.

Seeing Beth had poured each of them a glass, Elsa picked one up. "Here's to staying out of affairs of the heart." She turned toward Deanna. "I'm sorry to put you in an awkward situation. Obviously, my son has gained some sense when it comes to choosing his love interest since moving to Aspen Cove."

"I'll drink to that." Merrick lifted his glass. "The part about you staying out of my love life." He wrapped his free arm around Deanna and tugged her close to him. "I definitely picked the right girl this time."

"Hey," she said. "I think I picked you."

He took a sip of his wine. "Then, that proves you have good taste."

The next hour she nursed a glass that never seemed to empty due to Beth the ninja wine pourer, and by the time the sun fully set, she was mostly toast.

"I made up your room with clean sheets," Elsa said, looking at Merrick. "Why don't you two stay the night." She turned to face Deanna. "Merrick is off, and hopefully, you have a flexible schedule that allows you to hang out for the rest of the night with us and leave tomorrow. It's not often I have both of my children at home."

Deanna had just enough wine to be accommodating.

"I do a lot of my work remotely. Right now, work is slow. The band is finishing up an album, and then they are going on hiatus until the first of the year." She leaned in as if telling a secret. "There's been a lot of pregnancies in Aspen Cove. It's like some contagion, and I think Samantha has it. If I'm right, I bet she'll be expecting before the end of the year."

Elsa bounced up and down on her chair. "Oh, I hope it's contagious." She looked between her children. "One of you has to give me a grandchild while I'm young enough to enjoy him or her."

Beth raised her hands in surrender. "Don't look at me. I don't even have a boyfriend unless Deanna can fix me up with one of her musicians. I rather like that one they call Red."

Merrick let out a growl that scared Sherman. He dashed from his hiding place under Deanna's feet and jumped in Elsa's lap.

"Oh my." Elsa laughed and snuggled the dog to her chest. "I take it you don't like this Red?"

Dislike was a kind word for what she knew

Merrick felt for the man. If he didn't want her, a woman he barely knew, with the sexy bass player, he'd never let his sister get with him.

"The man isn't worthy of any of you." He stared straight at Deanna. "Especially you." He turned to face his sister before the word was finished, but Deanna knew his words were meant for her.

Feeling the day catch up to her, she raised her arms in a stretch. "While I'd love to stay up and chat, the wine has gone straight to my head and settled in my sleep zone. If you don't mind, I'll take Sherman out to do his business and head to bed. Where would you like me to sleep?"

Elsa laughed. "With Merrick, of course. I know you kids have a three-date rule, which I'm sure you've already surpassed. You don't have to play celibate to stay at my house. Besides, Beth is staying in her room, so I'm all out of beds. That works, right?" She lifted those soul-searching brows again.

"Perfect." Deanna cleared her throat. "I just wanted to respect your house rules." The blood pumped through her veins. When she stood, she stumbled, but Merrick caught her.

"Is it the wine?" His eyes danced with mischief. "Or something else?"

"Oh, it's something all right."

Merrick grabbed Sherman from Elsa's arms. "Good night, Mom." He turned to his sister. "See you in the morning runt." With the dog in one arm and the other wrapped around her waist, he led her to the backyard where Sherman was quick to do his business and hop back into Merrick's arms.

"Traitor," Deanna said under her breath. "I swear that dog likes no one but me and you Buchanans."

Merrick chuckled. "Not true, he likes just about everyone but Red. Remember what I told you, always trust dogs and children." He kissed the top of her head as he walked her up the stairs. "Ready for bed, babe?"

CHAPTER THIRTEEN

The last time Merrick walked into his childhood home with a girl was when he snuck Theresa Browning in after school. They only got to second base before his mother caught him. It was the most embarrassing moment of his life.

As he entered, he realized not much had changed. The walls were still covered in sports posters and the shelves in trophies.

He closed the door behind them and set Sherman on the floor. The dog sniffed around and settled next to the beanbag in the corner.

"Oh my God," Deanna whispered. "Your mother thinks we're …"

"We're what?" He was enjoying her discomfort and found it cute that she got embarrassed. Especially when she was so bold as to pull him, a stranger, in for the best kiss of his life not too long ago.

"Sleeping together."

He bit his lip and shook his head. "When we finally climb into bed together ... there will be no sleep."

Her jaw dropped open, and he used his index finger to lift her chin and shut it. "Don't tease me with that open mouth, babe. You're giving me ideas."

Her cheeks turned hot crimson red. It was a good look on her.

"Merrick, what the hell are we going to do?"

He looked past her to the bed. "Seems to me like the best plan of attack is to get undressed and climb between the sheets."

"You're kidding, right?"

He walked up to her until they were chest to chest. He liked that she was taller than most women. Appreciated that he didn't have to put a kink in his neck to kiss her.

With his lips close to hers but not touching, he said, "Relax. I'm not asking you to sleep with me."

Immediately her head cocked like a confused puppy. "You're not?"

He placed his hands on her shoulders and stepped her back until the mattress hit her knees, and they buckled, taking her to a seated position on the edge of the bed.

"No, I'm not."

"Why not? What's wrong with me?" There was an almost plaintiff begging to her voice. One that nearly dropped him to his knees in front of her.

"There's nothing wrong with you. You're perfect." *For me.*

"Then why don't you want me?" She flopped onto her back and stared at the ceiling.

"It's not a matter of want, Deanna. It's about respect and honor. I am not who you want, and I refuse to be a stand-in for some asshole that doesn't deserve you."

She rolled to her side. "You're right. He doesn't deserve me."

"Glad we finally agree." He moved to his dresser and pulled out a T-shirt. He always kept a few things here in case he needed them. "You can wear this." He pointed to a door she hadn't seen. "There's a bathroom there. It connects with Beth's room, so don't be surprised if she walks in on you. She's famous for not knocking." He tossed her the shirt.

"Do you have something to wear?"

He decided to mess with her some more. "I sleep in the nude."

Her eyes shot to his, and they lowered to his

groin. She stared at him so long he felt the heat of her gaze seep past his denim.

"You're sleeping in the nude in the bed next to me?" She touched her forehead. "I have to tell you, Merrick, a girl can only take so much."

He offered her his hand and yanked her to her feet. "Go get dressed." He turned her toward the bathroom door and gave her a swat on the backside.

With a yelp and a giggle, she skipped forward and disappeared behind the door.

"What the hell am I going to do about that woman?" he mumbled. "There's a spare toothbrush in the drawer," he called out loud enough for her to hear.

"Thank you," she answered back.

While she changed and readied herself for bed, he slipped out of his clothes and into an old pair of sweats. Though he usually didn't wear anything to bed, to go nude in a room where Deanna only wore a T-shirt wasn't wise. He liked her far too much not to want her. Her words replayed in his mind. "What's wrong with me?" Nothing was wrong with her, and that was a problem. He wanted her in the worst way possible, but not for a single encounter. He was an always man, and in his experience, always only lasted until someone better came along.

By the time she entered his room, he had laid a blanket on the floor and was using the beanbag as a pillow. It wasn't comfortable, but he'd slept in worse places.

"What are you doing down there?"

"I'm a gentleman. Now climb in bed and go to sleep."

"I thought you were sleeping with me."

"Told you, if I were in that bed, you'd get no sleep."

He sat up, and the cover dropped from his shoulders to expose his chest.

Her eyes grew wide.

He knew attraction when he saw it. Deanna was as drawn to him as he was to her.

"You're not going to get much sleep on the floor."

"Go to bed, Deanna." His voice came out sterner than he planned.

"Are you mad at me?"

"No. Now shut off the light and climb into bed."

She let out a huff and moved toward the door where she flicked the switch off. But even in the dark, he could see her outline cut from the light of the moon peeking in the window—small waist, round hips, and legs that went on forever.

What started as heat in his groin turned into an insistent throbbing.

The swish of the sheets pushed the scent of her

perfume through the air. Its sweet smell drifted through the room to mix with everything else about her that turned him on. He let out a groan and turned his back to temptation.

"You okay?" she asked.

He didn't answer but let the silence sit between them.

Just when the heat of his desire ebbed, she spoke. "Merrick?"

He took in a deep breath and let the exhale whistle out. "What do you need, Deanna?"

She was silent for a stretch, and he was certain she'd fallen asleep, but then her voice, the barest of whispers, broke the quiet. "I need you. Come to bed with me."

His heart pounded so hard he was convinced his pecs would hurt from the beating. "If I climb in that bed, you know what's going to happen." He waited for her reply. Expected her to come to her senses.

"Come to bed, Merrick. Let's not make a liar out of your mother."

He flew from the floor and climbed in next to her. "My mother has no place in this bed. It's you and me. If I stay beside you tonight, it's just us. Okay?"

"Just us." She reached out to trace her fingers over his chest.

Like a bolt of lightning, her touch charged him. "Make sure this is what you want." His hands shook to touch her, but he needed her to reconfirm her desire. "This has to be you talking, not the wine. You have to want me. Not just a stand-in for someone else."

"I want you."

He pulled her into his arms and nuzzled her neck. "You've got me, babe. I'm all yours."

When their lips met, it was like he was kissing her for the first time. Maybe that was because this time, it all felt real. Like somehow, during their make-believe love affair, something genuine had transpired.

He nipped at her bottom lip until she gasped, then sucked it between his lips until she moaned. When she pressed her hips into his, he did the same, showing her how aroused she made him feel.

"Merrick?"

"Deanna?" He said a silent prayer that she wasn't calling this off. That she hadn't come to her senses and decided he should go back to the floor.

"Take your sweats off."

Thank the heavens. He shimmied out of his pants while she pulled her shirt over her head. God, she was beautiful. He didn't have the light of day to see her, but the shadowed outline of perfect breasts and a body was enough. He promised himself he would do his best to rock her world.

He took his time with her. Something told him that Deanna had been sorely neglected by the men she dated. Any woman who settled for an asshole like Red didn't know she could ask for more. It was his job to show her what more was.

He spent endless minutes on her mouth before moving his way down to worship her breasts. Lord, she had fabulous breasts. Not the overstuffed, never budged from their spot, surgically enhanced type, but the kind that filled a palm to perfection.

Her skin tasted like a sweet dessert, and the moans that slipped from her lips were like music. As her body started to tremble, he knew she was close, and he hadn't even arrived at the good stuff.

One subtle kiss to her core sent her soaring, and when she came down, he sent her over the edge one more time before he took his place cradled between her thighs.

He was wrong. It wasn't him who rocked her world but her who destroyed his. That one time was all it took to fall head over heels in love with Deanna.

When they lay sated in each other's arms, he pressed his lips to her damp forehead. "I want to do that again."

"Are you serious?"

"I promised you all night."

"That you did." She snuggled into his body. "Are you a man of your word?"

"I never make a promise I can't keep."

As round two began, there was a pounding on the wall. "Keep it down in there. This girl needs her beauty sleep."

"Oh my God," Deanna said between giggles.

"Just ignore her."

He moved inside her, feeling the connection between them build until he fell over the edge. In his post-coital bliss, he reached out and pulled her to him. She fit against him like every one of his muscles was designed for her curves.

Words of love were on the tip of his tongue, but as he held her close and opened his mouth to tell her how much he'd come to care for her, she said, "At least our story is solid. No one would believe we're not the real thing now."

CHAPTER FOURTEEN

When Deanna woke up, she was alone. The residual heat from Merrick's missing body was the only thing that confirmed she hadn't slept alone. That and the delicious soreness that pulled at every muscle.

She flopped onto her back and relived the night in her mind. Merrick had done things to her she'd never experienced. How was it this man could make her feel so good? Not just physically, but in every way. For a moment, it felt real. In fact, she'd thrown it out there last night and made an offhanded comment that no one would believe they weren't a genuine couple, but he didn't take the bait. He didn't tell her she was wrong, and they were indeed together for real. Nope, he gave her pleasure, took his own, and then he rolled over and fell asleep. The arms she hoped to wake up to were gone.

Merrick seemed different from all the others, but he wasn't. Men were all the same. They got what they wanted and moved on. What made last night any different from her time with Red?

The sex was better last night. So much better.

She threw off the covers and gathered her clothes. "What's wrong with me?" She entered the bathroom and turned on the shower. Sherman took a seat next to the sink like he did at home. She looked at him. "You're the only loyal man in my life, and that's because I buy your favorite kibble."

Once under the water, she let the heated stream sluice over her sore muscles. "Why couldn't this be real?" She stuck her face under the water and let the tears come. All she wanted was someone to love her. Having sex, as wonderful as it could be, wasn't love. It was just about perfect last night, but waking up alone reminded her that she'd offered another man everything, and he took what he wanted and left.

Fifteen minutes later, she was downstairs, standing on the back patio watching Sherman chase a rabbit. Maybe this was what her life would be like. She wouldn't be a single woman with a bunch of cats, but perhaps the only true love she'd experience was that of a loyal dog.

"Good morning," Beth walked out of the house carrying two cups of coffee. She offered one to Deanna.

The first sip was so good. It had the perfect ratio of cream to sugar. "How did you know?"

"Merrick told me. He said you liked it strong and sweet, like your men, but toned down with a splash of cream."

"He did, huh?" How could a man be so considerate to remember her coffee but not stay in bed to say good morning? "Where is Merrick?" That was the question of the day.

"He's helping Mom load up her car. She's doing a free book fair at the homeless shelter and needed to borrow my brother's muscles." She leaned on a nearby rail. "Sounded to me like you both got plenty of exercise last night."

"Oh my God, don't go there." Her face had to be red since she could feel the flame-like heat on her cheeks. "I'm not talking about what happened last night." She was still processing it herself. There was great joy followed by severe disappointment.

"I want what you two have."

Deanna wanted to scream,—*We have nothing!*— but she wouldn't do that to Merrick. They had an agreement, and she'd stick to her part of the bargain.

However, she wouldn't hold him to his. All this make-believe made her believe.

"You'll find your prince."

"Are you sure you can't introduce me to Red?"

"I could, but then your brother would be forced to commit murder, and I'm sure that goes against his whole serve and protect persona."

"Why all the color names for the band? What happened to Axel? Is Samantha as pretty in person? Did her husband really kill someone?" She rambled off several questions before taking a deep breath.

"Um, Red's name is really Red. Gray is actually Gary. I think he and Red made a bet of some sort, and Gary lost, and that's how come he changed it to Gray. Something about Gary being boring. Axel's name is Alex, and he hooked up with the school-teacher and found out he has a five-year-old daughter. He's been fully domesticated since Mercy came into his life. Samantha's beautiful inside and out, and yes, Dalton killed someone, but it was because he was protecting a woman. It's not what the press made it out to be."

"I bet my brother would kill anyone who tried to do you harm. I've never seen him look at a woman the way he looks at you."

He's a good actor. "Your brother is a good man." There were times when she said things, and they didn't feel right, but that was a statement that felt solid. Merrick was good. He just wasn't her man. Her heart became heavy at the realization that she had fallen for Merrick while she was chasing Red.

"I've always known that, and I'm glad he found you because you are perfect for each other."

"As I said, he's one of the good ones."

"Do you love him?"

"Love?" This was getting far too complicated. "It's way too early for love. I hardly know him."

She narrowed her eyes. "I call bullshit. I can see your affection toward him in every look you send his way. What I see is love."

"I suppose you'll see what you want to see. You love your brother and want him to be loved."

The door opened, and a shadow fell across them. "What about love?" Merrick's deep voice vibrated against her skin, and every hair stood up like they were begging for his touch.

Beth turned to face her brother, but Deanna continued to stare into the yard. Facing him seemed an impossible task. She had to get her feelings in check before she could plaster a look of disinterest on her face. Anything less than void would show him how much his dismissal of her hurt. She was tired of men stomping on her heart.

"I was telling Deanna that I've never seen two people more in love with each other. I adore seeing this soft side of my brother."

Deanna turned to face them, hoping she'd compartmentalized her feelings.

He let out a sigh. "Don't reserve the church just yet." He knuckled the top of Beth's head, which sent her running into the house.

Once Beth was gone, he turned to her. "Mom asked us to stay for lunch, but I told her we needed to get back, so as soon as you're ready, I think we'll hit the road. I can go through a drive-thru on the way to get a burger or whatever you want to eat."

"Oh, umm, okay. Let me get my bag and feed Sherman, and then I'll be ready."

He shoved his hands inside his pockets and looked at the ground. "Thanks for everything."

Part of her wanted to smile at the little boy inside the man, but the other part of her wanted to slap him upside the head. He was acting like she gave him a lollipop when she gave him so much more than that.

"Yep," she slid past him. "Glad I could help."

Before she could escape, he reached out and touched her arm. The touch tingled all the way to the pit of her stomach. "Do you want to talk about last night?"

She shook her head. "Nope. It was a mistake. A good mistake, but honestly, that shouldn't have happened."

When she looked up, his eyes bore into hers. "I wouldn't call it a mistake."

"It wasn't the objective or part of the plan. It just happened."

His jaw hardened, and his lips thinned. "Right, the plan." He dropped his hand from her arm. "Best to keep with the plan."

"Right," she said and walked inside the house, feeling worse than she did when she slid off the hood of Red's car that night. As she marched up the stairs, she considered her choice of men. Red and Merrick were polar opposites, but they were twins when it came to women and commitment. They were happy inside a woman's body but never interested in living in her heart.

She made the bed because this wasn't a hotel, and Merrick's mother wasn't their maid. She picked up her bag and fetched Sherman. Elsa walked into the house just as she exited.

"I'm so sad you two can't stay for lunch. Merrick said you have a busy schedule. Something about a project for work you need to complete."

The only project she knew about was Red, but at this point, she was done with men, Red included. Dogs were so much easier. They loved you unconditionally, and they rarely complained when you got home late or didn't have supper ready at a specific time. They never snuck out of bed before daybreak.

"Yes, sorry about that."

Elsa pulled her in for a hug. "I'm so glad you're part of the family now. Let's keep it that way."

She hated to string Merrick's mom along. It hardly seemed fair to make her believe there was hope for them when all hope was lost. "You're a lovely family. Thank you for your hospitality."

"We'll see you soon." She kissed Deanna on the cheek and walked inside.

Deanna situated Sherman in the back seat and climbed into the passenger's side to wait for Merrick. He came out with Beth, his arm wrapped around her protectively. She'd miss that arm and all the times it draped over her shoulder.

Beth opened the door and flung herself toward Deanna. "I'm coming to Aspen Cove to visit. I expect you to set me up on that date with the bass player."

"Your brother is right. He's not a good guy."

Merrick had climbed inside in time to hear her comment. "But women love him anyway. What's with the attraction to bad boys? They don't value you, they rarely show up emotionally, and they treat you like crap."

"It's like taming a wild horse," Beth said with a

giggle. "Few people can do it, but it doesn't stop you from trying."

"Red is off-limits. Listen to Deanna. He's not a good guy. She should know. She dated him."

Beth's jaw dropped. "You dated Red?"

Deanna was ready to choke Merrick. "No, I didn't date him, I just ... let's say this. Like you, I found him attractive, but men like Red can't be tamed."

"We'll see." Beth turned around and walked away.

"Why would you tell her that?"

He backed out of the driveway, and they headed for Aspen Cove.

"Why wouldn't I? Beth is hardheaded, and if she thinks she's got an in to meet Red, she's going to take it. Every family has a saint and a sinner. I'm the one with the wings."

"Don't fool yourself. You're no angel."

CHAPTER FIFTEEN

"And then she told me I was no angel."

Cannon filled Merrick's mug and slid it across the bar.

"Don't ask me for love advice. It took me forever to get Sage to say yes, and when she did, it took her another lifetime for her to say I do. I suck in matters of the heart." He nodded toward the end of the bar, where Doc sat sipping his beer. "He's Dr. Love. I mean ... any man who has been around as many decades as he has, knows something about women and hearts."

"I'm not after her heart." *But she managed to bruise mine.*

"That's your problem," Doc said. "You young'uns don't know how to woo a woman. You think romance is a dinner out, a glass of wine, and a roll in the hay, but for women, romance begins in the head and lodges in the heart before their feminine parts ever get involved." He patted the stool beside him. "Come on over." He lifted his half-empty mug toward Cannon. "Put this and the next one on his tab."

Merrick looked around the nearly empty bar. He wasn't usually a day drinker, but after dropping Deanna off, he headed straight for Bishop's Brewhouse. The silent drive back gnawed at his insides. He wanted to ask her so many things, like why he wasn't enough, but he stayed quiet and sulked all the way home while she stared out the window. Even Sherman picked up on the mood and refused a pet when they arrived. The scrawny poodle ran past him and straight to the door.

He and Doc were the only patrons, but in a few hours, it would be bustling with every off-work resident and the crews in town working diligently to remodel or rebuild the derelict houses left behind. Right now, it smelled like lemon oil and pine cleaner, but by six, it would be a mix of sweat, spilled beer, and cologne. That was probably why Doc was here now.

"I think I owe you one anyway," Merrick said as he slid over several stools to take a seat next to Doc.

"I believe you do." Doc crumbled up his half-played tic-tac-toe game and tossed the wadded napkin toward the trash can but missed and ended up hitting Mike, Cannon's one-eyed cat, instead. Mike didn't seem fazed. He stayed right where he was on the back counter, swishing his tail like he didn't have a care in the world.

Doc lifted his hand and turned over an imaginary sign. "The Doc is in. Tell me what's on your mind, son."

"Nothing, really."

Doc shook his head. Those bushy brows of his lifted like wings, ready to take flight. "Lying to yourself is useless. You've got the greatest bullshit detector inside you. It's called a conscience. Not everyone has one, but you do."

"How do you know?"

"I got a glimpse of it during our last counseling session."

"Is this what we're calling these impromptu meetings?"

Doc chuckled. "We're not dating, so what else would you call it?"

Merrick lifted his beer and took two gulps. "It's Deanna."

The older man stared at his beer for several long seconds. "I told you before, women don't bring you peace, son, they bring you everything else from happiness to hurt but rarely peace."

"That you did."

"You like the girl?"

"I liked her then, although, I didn't know her well, but I've been lucky enough to spend some time with her, and she's amazing."

Doc narrowed his eyes. "When you say spend some time with her, are you talking long walks around the lake or a short tumble between the sheets? I hear you youngsters have some three-date rule."

Didn't his mother say something similar? "Doc, I'm not going to kiss and tell."

"I respect that." Doc took a sip of his beer and licked the foam from his lip. "What's the rush? You ever have a Thanksgiving dinner, and you rushed through the main course to get to the pumpkin pie." He smoothed his mustache with his thumb and index finger. "I prefer apple, but that's not what we're talking about."

"What are we talking about?"

"We're discussing the importance of taking your time to enjoy all the flavors. Savor each dish a woman serves you—a walk in the park is the appetizer. Then you have to work your way through the stuffing and green bean casserole and sweet potato bake. You move on to the mashed potatoes and gravy, the cranberry sauce, the turkey, and the hot cross buns. You cherish each bite like it's a destination all on its own. Sometimes it's better to sit back and wait for dessert. That's all I'm saying."

He understood exactly what Doc meant. Back in his day, they wooed a woman. Nowadays, there was this need for instant gratification.

"Do you think she regretted indulging in dessert first?"

"Son, I've got no idea. What about you? Do you have regrets?"

He found his head nodding before his brain even processed the question. "I do. Not because I didn't enjoy the decadence, but because ... I wasn't the dessert she was craving."

"Still that Red fellow, huh?"

He nodded and sat there without saying a word for several minutes. It was in the silence that the weight of the loss got heavy.

"Are you the fish or the pole? The fox or the rabbit?"

Memories of their first conversation came flooding back, and he had to wonder if he'd approached this whole thing wrong. What Deanna wanted was for someone to want her. She hated that Red didn't pursue her.

"I made a big mistake, Doc."

"We all do, son. We all do. That's how we grow. The question is, what did you learn from it?"

He emptied his mug. "I need to be the fisherman and not the fish." Merrick slapped a twenty on the table. "I've got to go. My tackle box needs some upgrades."

"Pay careful attention to the bait, son. Don't offer something amazing if you can't sustain it."

"Right." Walking away, energy rippled through his cells. A rush of adrenaline spiked in his blood. He wasn't a damn fish, but last night when he made love to Deanna, it was she who threw the line and bait into the water. He was hooked and reeled in. While he loved that she wanted him, he needed her to want only him.

He stepped into the sunshine and felt its warmth on his face. He'd done a lot wrong with Deanna. She was a woman worth fighting for, and nobody, to his knowledge, had, and that was going to change.

She might think she wanted Red, but he'd prove to her that he wasn't the full meal she needed. He wasn't even dessert. Red was an appetizer and a poor one at that. He was the flavorless garnish that always got left on the plate.

On his way home, he considered all the ways someone could show affection. Sure, there were flowers and candy and nights out on the town, but those left with the wilting of a daisy, the consumption of the candy, and the time since the last date. He needed to do something big. Something that would remind her daily that he would be there fighting for her.

He pulled into his driveway and looked at his garden. It was a source of pride and made his house look like a home. He recalled Deanna telling him her house was an eyesore. He couldn't restore her old money pit, but he could make it welcoming. If he split the plants that were overgrowing in his yard like daylilies and irises, he wouldn't have to pick up too much.

When he moved in, he at least had a garden to work with. Deanna had a patch of dead grass and weeds. Though it was fall and the fruits of his labor wouldn't be fully realized until spring, he knew he could make a difference.

His first call was to the only man in town who had a green thumb, his boss, Aiden.

"Sheriff Cooper, how can I help you?" Aiden answered.

"Hey Coop, it's Merrick. Do you still have those perennials you offered me when I moved in?" Aiden was a gardener at heart and planted and tilled from the first sign of spring until the frost hardened the ground, or so he was told. He grew the best tomatoes, the biggest zucchini, and if his daughter, Kellyn, was right, a pumpkin large enough to turn into a carriage. He mentally crossed his fingers and hoped the answer was yes.

"I've got tons of sedum, a few lavender plants I can spare, and a couple of salvias. Are you expanding your yard?"

"Nope, I'm being neighborly. Deanna's yard is barren, and I thought if I could plant some things into the ground now, they'd have time to establish roots before the first frost."

"It's pushing it, but as long as you amend the soil and make sure they get water during the months we lack precipitation, then I think it can work. How about I bring what I have by later? You want me to drop it off at your house or hers?"

"Mine. This is a surprise."

"Things going well in that department?"

"Nope, not really, so I'm going with a different approach."

Aiden chuckled. "I won Marina over by transforming her garden overnight. I waited until she and Kellyn went to bed, and then I went to work. When she woke up, everything had changed."

Could everything change? "You're an inspiration."

"I'm a lovesick fool." In the background, the squeak of Aiden's chair filled the air. "It's never too late to be kind. What I've found is if you make people feel love, they give love."

That was the universal truth to everything. Reap what you sow, and tomorrow, while she was at work, he would sow irises and daylilies and sedum into the soil and hopefully plant himself in Deanna's good graces.

As he pulled out a pad of paper and a pen to sketch out a plan, a seed of doubt tried to sprout. *Was this all for nothing?*

He buried that thought. Even if his actions didn't move their friendship forward, Deanna was part of Aspen Cove, and the community motto was: "This is Aspen Cove, and we take care of our own."

CHAPTER SIXTEEN

The mockups of the covers were on the third round. There was always someone who didn't like something. While Samantha was sweet and friendly, she was often too accommodating. Why wouldn't she be? A failed plan didn't create more work for her.

Deanna hated the bitterness that was seeping into the crevices of her life. She grabbed her keys and walked to the door.

"Behave yourself," she told Sherman. While she usually took him with her, she feared that if he tried to bite Red, she wouldn't stop him. She was tempted to sprinkle him with bacon fat to entice Sherman. Nothing good could come out of that.

Most of the day was eaten up by her trip to Copper Creek to pick up the proofs delivered later than she anticipated. She made the return drive to the Guild Creative Center and parked in the back. In the parking lot, Sosie Grant was unloading blank canvases from the back of Baxter's truck.

"I'll get the door," Deanna said and rushed ahead to open it for the artist. "How are you?"

Sosie smiled. She had that look of bliss about her. It was an ethereal glow that seemed to float around her like a halo.

"I'm good but busy. It seems as if everyone wants a Sosie Grant original these days. It's always feast or famine, isn't it? One day you have it all, and the next, you've got nothing." She giggled. "Right now, I have it all, and I'm willing to make a deal with the Devil to keep it."

Deanna knew she was joking about the deal with the Devil. "I don't want it all. I just want some of it." She had no idea what the feast part of feast or famine looked like unless it was an overindulgence in Hostess pies. "A little piece of good would satisfy me."

Sosie wheeled the cart past her and into the hallway. "Not true. It's like having one potato chip. You lie to yourself and say you'll only eat one, but that single bite is never enough, and before you know it, you hate yourself because you ate the whole bag."

"But what if you're only offered a single chip?"

Sosie laughed, "The one thing I've learned from losing my sight and getting it back is that until you can satisfy yourself, be truly happy with you, no one will be able to offer you enough." She unlocked her studio door and pushed the cart of canvases inside. "However, if someone offers you less than what you want ... move on. You deserve to have everything you want and need from a relationship." She parked the cart and faced Deanna. "We were talking about men, right?"

"You're far too intuitive, and that was solid advice." It was what her brain had been telling her all day. She needed to focus on her needs for once. Define what she wanted from herself and a relationship. "Do you need help with anything?" She looked at the mockups in her hand. "I can drop these off and be back in a few."

Sosie shook her head. "Nope, I appreciate you opening the door. There are times when I think having more than two hands would be wise."

"Wouldn't that be awesome?" As she walked down the hallway to the recording studio, she passed the other artists' spaces. There was a welder who created unique metal art. She was Baxter's sister and Dalton's cousin. One unit was rented to a sculptor, but, to her knowledge, he hadn't been in town for a while. The gallery was filled with Poppy Bancroft's photos of the residents. They were how Deanna put the names to the faces.

She moved past Dalton's Culinary Kitchen and took in the smell of pasta sauce. She loved the days when Dalton cooked spaghetti. He made it from Roma tomatoes and fresh spices. Nothing honestly tasted as good as his sauce over pasta and served with a side of meatballs.

She stuck her head in the door and found him at the prep table. "I'll take a pint of sauce and the rest of whatever you're making."

He nodded. "I already put you down for a hefty helping. Will you have company?" He lifted a brow.

"Nope, I'm solo for a while."

"That's too bad. I thought things were going well with you and—"

"I'm done with Red."

Dalton snapped his head back like she'd slapped him. "I was going to say Merrick. You and Red?" He shook his head. "I don't see that happening."

"Your vision is twenty-twenty. It isn't happening." She lifted the artwork. "I got to go piss people off." She knew she was in for another round of complaints and wasn't in the mood.

"I'll have your dinner waiting for when you leave."

"You're the best."

"I keep telling Samantha that. I've almost got her believing it."

Deanna rolled her eyes. "Oh, please. That girl is head over stilettos for you."

"It's because I can cook."

"You got a brother?" She pushed off the door and walked away before he could answer. She already knew he was an only child.

At the end of the hallway was the recording studio. As she walked in, she heard the familiar bass of "Another One Bites the Dust." Maybe that should be her theme song.

"Hey," Samantha walked over and hugged her. "Did you get the cover art back?"

"I did." She held out the mockups. "Before you show everyone, I wanted to say that you're the boss, so in the end, it's your choice."

Samantha smiled. "I know, but I like it when everyone is on the same page."

Samantha didn't like conflict. She wasn't afraid to address it, but that didn't mean she had to deal with it.

"Okay, all I'm saying is the artist is ready to toss in the towel, so if we come back with more changes, we'll probably have to find someone else."

Samantha frowned. "How many times have we asked for amendments?"

"Gray didn't like the sun in the background and Red wasn't fond of the shade of blue."

"It's always indigo blue."

"I know, but he thinks next to the yellow, it's taking on a different hue. Then he wasn't a fan of the way your hair blew out and covered their faces, so you chose that picture where you have the high ponytail, but then you were almost as tall as them."

Samantha laughed. "I'm five foot, nearly nothing. I'd have to be wearing stilts to be that tall." She took the graphics and headed for the studio. "Okay, I've got this." They walked to the door, but before she opened it, Samantha faced her. "You okay? You seem off. Did something happen with Red again?"

Her face scrunched up the way a kid's face did when they ate a lemon.

"Nope."

"Merrick?"

"Geez, you make it sound like I've got a reverse harem."

She laughed. "Well, you do have two of the hottest guys in town fighting for you."

That was the biggest laugh of all. "No one is fighting for me. There's no Red or Merrick. I'm an island."

"No one is ever really an island." Samantha turned the knob and walked inside. "Look, guys, Deanna brought us the final cover. She's tired of our bullshit." Samantha looked at Red when she uttered the last word. "This is it. You love it or leave it."

She held it up, and everyone nodded but Red.

"It's still the wrong blue," he said.

Deanna was fed up with him. She grabbed the closest weapon, which happened to be an empty box from the bakery. She stomped toward Red and hit him over the head with it. "What's your problem? Nothing is ever good enough for you. You take and take and never give back. When will your soul-sucking neediness be sated!"

She whacked him once more, then spun around and fled the room.

She was halfway to her car when a hand landed on her shoulder. She turned to find Red behind her.

"Back away, or I might hurt you."

He rubbed his head. "You already gave me a concussion."

"Yeah, well, you give me a headache and indigestion."

"No, that's from those cherry pies you eat all the time."

She had no idea he paid attention. "Well, I need one right now. Leave me alone."

"I don't know why you're so mad at me. I thought you liked me."

She stepped back. "I used to, but you know what? I can't imagine what I ever saw in you."

"Are you still with that baboon?"

"Merrick?" She was done with the ruse. "I was never with Merrick. You were right. I used him to make you jealous. He used me to get his mom off his case. She wants a grandkid."

Red laughed. "I knew it." He moved a step closer. "How about I get a bottle of wine and come over later?"

"Are you nuts?" She tapped him on his head. "Did someone drop you on your head as a child?" She turned and headed for the back door. "All I wanted was to love you, but love isn't a one-way road. You don't need my love when you have the adoration of hundreds of women. Besides, you love yourself enough that you don't require it from anyone else. But you know what? I need love. I need someone to want me and fight for me. For the first time in a long time, I realize that person will never be you."

"Oh, come on, Deanna. You knew who I was, and you wanted me anyway." He followed her to her car.

Beth's words rang in her head. *It's like taming a wild horse. Few people can do it, but it doesn't stop you from trying.*

"I'm done wanting you."

"No, you're not. You're not a quitter." He leaned in as if he would kiss her, but she pushed him away, hard enough to send him staggering backward.

"There's a difference between quitting and knowing when the prize isn't worth the effort."

She climbed into her car and drove back home. As she rounded the corner to her street, she found Merrick in her front yard with a shovel.

She pulled into her driveway and got out.

"What are you doing?"

Merrick walked up to her. "I'm being neighborly."

"Are you insane?" She seemed to be asking that a lot lately. "Why are you in my yard?"

He looked over his shoulder, where several flower beds had been tilled and planted.

"I wanted you to have something you wanted."

She glared at him. "You and I both know I can't have what I want." She marched past him and into the house.

As she closed the door, she heard his response. "Maybe you should stop wanting what you can't have."

She slammed the door the rest of the way, and for the next hour, she paced the floor, catching glimpses of Merrick as he prettied up her yard.

Seeing him was like picking at a scab and then pouring salt on the wound.

Why couldn't anyone love her the way she deserved to be loved? In her head, she heard Merrick tell her that she deserved more, and he was right.

She was done with men ... all men.

CHAPTER SEVENTEEN

Hot and sweaty and pissed off, Merrick trudged into his house.

"What the hell is her problem?" He headed straight to the shower to wash off the dirt and grime. "I was just being nice and giving her something beautiful to come home to."

That was why staying single was wise. Women were trouble. He knew better than to believe he could find love. When something seemed too good to be true, it generally was. Once clean, he changed into jeans and walked to Bishop's Brewhouse. All he wanted was to drown in beer. He didn't need any more of Doc's advice or that of his boss, Aiden. He needed about three rounds of beer to numb his agitation.

When he arrived, Doc was sitting at the bar, sipping his daily brew. If Merrick didn't have bad luck, he wouldn't have any. What were the chances of him coming at all different times of the day and finding Doc as if he were waiting for him?

He turned as Merrick walked inside the door.

"Uh-oh, you look like you could use a drink." Doc knocked on the bar, which brought Cannon out from the back room.

"You look like shit, man. What happened to you?" Cannon asked.

Merrick's palms came to his face to rub at his eyes. Not only did digging in Deanna's garden give him blisters, but the damn weeds kicked up his allergies, making him want to claw out his own eyes.

"I'm fine."

"No, he isn't," Doc said. "Have a seat, son." He pointed to the stool next to him and then to the tap. "Cannon, pour the boy a beer."

"I'll need three," Merrick added.

Doc shook his head and turned to face him. "He'll take them one at a time."

"I'm not in the mood for your sage advice today. No more talk about fishing lines and bait and rabbits and foxes. All I want is to drink until I'm numb and then go home and pass out."

"What you want and what you're getting are two vastly different things." Doc picked up his beer and took a sip. "You came into my office, and that means you'll listen to what I've got to say."

"Your office? This is a damn bar."

Doc lifted his hand and pretended to turn over his make-believe sign. "The doctor is in. Now tell me, what the hell has your knickers in a twist?"

"Women."

"Women in general or a particular one?" Doc asked.

Cannon pulled the beer and set it on the bar in front of Merrick. "Oh, man. Can't live with them and can't live without them. Lord knows you can't please them. Just this morning, Sage handed me a note outlining five things I wasn't allowed to say right now." He pulled the note from his pocket. "I kept it with me so I could memorize it."

"Only five things," Doc asked.

"Isn't five enough? Listen to these. In no partic-ular order they are:

It's not so bad.

It feels like you've been pregnant forever.

Are you eating those candy bars again?

I know how you feel.

I'm in the mood."

"Sage is a wise woman to give you the informa-tion in the way a man needs it. Most women hint at things or expect us to know what they want, but the reality is, men are clueless. Sage did you a favor by spelling it out. You've been schooled and warned all at once. If you screw it up and break her rules, which seem reasonable, it's your fault."

Merrick took several gulps of his beer. "Wouldn't it be nice if every woman came with a playbook?"

"What fun would that be?" Doc asked. "A relationship is like a present that gets delivered daily. Each morning you get up is like running to the Christmas tree to see what you got."

Doc was confusing. "Didn't you just tell Cannon that Sage did him a favor by giving him a list?"

"Cannon is hardheaded and needs a list. You, on the other hand, are good at reading people. The problem with Deanna is you're not speaking her language."

Cannon put a bowl of bar mix on the counter. "I'm not dense, and women aren't presents. They are more like onions, and you have to peel back the layers and hope they don't make you cry."

"Not a fan of onions and I haven't cried since I got my wisdom teeth removed. Hell, I got shot and never spilled a tear." Merrick glanced at Doc, who seemed to stare off into space, and that suited him just fine because if Doc's mind was elsewhere, he wouldn't be handing out advice like the male version of Dear Abby.

For a moment, he breathed in the tranquility of silence. The only sound in the place was the hum of the ice machine.

"What did you do that set her off?" Doc was back to being his nosy, annoying self. Merrick could almost feel his mother's hand, cuffing him upside the head and her voice telling him to respect his elders.

"I planted her a garden."

Cannon walked into the back room while Doc rubbed at his mustache. It was straight out of an old western with its business. It was a cross between Magnum PI and Wyatt Earp from *Tombstone*.

"Did you ask her if you could plant her a garden?"

What the hell was he talking about? "No, I didn't ask her. It was a surprise."

Doc picked through the bar mix and pulled all the peanuts out, leaving only the crackers for Merrick.

He popped one of the spicy rice ones into his mouth.

"Maybe she had other plans for her garden."

"I don't think she snapped at me because of the garden. I told her I wanted her to have something she wanted, and she yelled at me."

Doc lined up his peanuts in a row. "What did

she say?" He tossed one in the air and caught it in his mouth.

"She said that we both knew she couldn't have what she wanted, and then I yelled back that maybe she should stop wanting what she can't have."

"Hmm." Doc tossed two more peanuts into the air and caught them both. "You think this is about her wanting Red?"

Merrick tossed his arms into the air. "What else could it be about?"

Doc took his time eating the rest of his peanuts and taking several long gulps of his beer.

"In my experience, a woman won't put much effort toward a man she doesn't feel something for, and that means she won't put much emotion either. It seems to me Deanna is expending energy on you, and that doesn't make sense if she feels nothing. Have you seen how she's behaving around Red?"

He shook his head. The last thing he wanted to see was Deanna fawning over Red. "Maybe I'm wasting my energy worrying about it."

"Maybe, but perhaps you should put a little extra in to see where her passion lies. I mean, sit back and observe. It could be interesting."

"Not interested."

"Okay then," Doc emptied his beer. "All I can do is advise. You're the horse. I've led you to water. You can drink or not." Doc stood. And as he usually did, he let his bones creep back into place before he started for the door. "I'm assuming you're picking up the tab."

Merrick couldn't help but chuckle. "Do you ever pay for a beer in this place?"

Doc shook his head. "Not that often." He shuffled toward the door. "I hear that Maisey made her famous cherry pie today."

"And I want to know that because why?"

Doc made it to the door, then turned back. "First, it's good. Second, it's Deanna's favorite. I'm sure there's a third reason, but it escapes me." He moved out of the door.

Cannon returned from the hallway leading to the back room. "Is the coast clear?" He looked around for Doc.

"Yep, the wise one has left."

Cannon grabbed Doc's mug and washed it before putting it back into the freezer.

"You joke, but that man is the only reason I survived all these years. And because he works with Sage, he often gives me a heads up when I'm screwing something up."

Merrick turned his beer around and watched the liquid and bubbles stay in place. That was something explained by science that he didn't get. How could everything change, but what was on the inside remained the same?

"He said something to me about pie. I'm not sure how that's going to solve my problem."

Cannon shrugged. "Sweeten your disposition?"

"Me? Hell, I'm a regular sugar cube. Who needs pie?"

"Obviously, you do, or Doc wouldn't have mentioned it." Cannon swiped up Merrick's nearly empty mug. "Beers on me, go get your pie. Doc may or may not be right, but you'll never know unless you look."

When Merrick tried to put a twenty on the table, Cannon shook his head. "This one is on me. Doc's too. He already played me for his beer, and I lost."

"How often do you lose?"

"Almost every time, but I figure all the years of wisdom he extolled on me are worth something, and beer is the way I repay him."

Merrick nodded and rose from his seat. "Looks like I'm having some pie."

CHAPTER EIGHTEEN

Deanna was on her second piece of pie when Merrick passed by the window. She forked another bite and shoved it into her mouth as he entered the diner. There was no reason to be angry at him, but she was. Or maybe she was still mad at herself.

How many of the wrong men did she have to fall for before realizing that, if she liked them, they were terrible for her. This afternoon she decided to give up men and replace them with pie.

Merrick looked around the diner as he walked in. His gaze settled on her for a second. The entire place was empty, but he took the booth next to hers and sat, so he faced her.

She held up her half-empty plate to get

Maisey's attention. When the older woman walked over, Deanna said, "Maybe you should bring me the pie tin. I don't see me leaving here without devouring another piece. If I do that, I'm already in for half a pie. Maybe I should get the whole thing."

She looked between Merrick and Deanna. "I find that if I take a few minutes in between bites, I don't hate myself by the fourth piece."

"But this is only my second."

Maisey smiled and held up three fingers.

"No," Deanna said. "Seriously?"

Maisey nodded. "You still want the fourth?"

"No." She already hated herself for so many reasons. Not fitting into her jeans tomorrow didn't need to be another.

"I'll bring you back a cup of coffee to help wash everything down. When it all settles in your stomach, you'll feel that last piece. There's no doubt you'll feel the sugar rush." She turned toward Merrick, who seemed to be ingesting their conversation like she did pie—in big bites.

"Is there any pie left for me?"

"Sugar ... I've always got pie for the handsome ones."

Deanna made a *pffft* sound and rolled her eyes.

"You have something to say to me?" Merrick asked.

"Nope, not a thing."

He stared up at Maisey. "I'll take a piece of your famous cherry pie and a cup of coffee."

"Coming up."

Once Maisey was gone, it felt like something heavy sat in the room. She wanted to blame it on everything she ate, but it wasn't all internal. A proverbial white elephant was sitting between her and Merrick. It was hard to ignore.

He cleared his throat, which drew her attention from the last bite of pie on her plate.

"Did you need something?" she asked.

He shifted in the booth. Something told her he was ready to move, and she hoped it wasn't to her table. He lifted from his seat and walked toward her.

His cologne arrived before he did. The spicy mix floated below her nose and brought her back to the night at his mother's house. It was one of the best and worst nights of her life.

He plopped onto the bench across from her. "Yes, I need something. I need answers."

She moved a gooey cherry around her plate. She figured if she didn't look at him, she couldn't be drawn in by his lush lips, those soulful eyes, and the neatly trimmed beard that she knew she could still feel on her thighs if she just imagined hard enough.

Slowly, she lifted her chin and glanced at him. "I'm sorry I was short with you today."

"You call that short. You were like an atom bomb that detonated before you got there, and what I got was the fallout. All I was trying to do was something nice." He sucked in a breath, which expanded his chest. "What? You don't like daylilies and irises. Do you have something against sedum?"

"No, it's not that. Look, I had a bad day at work. People are always pushing me in directions I don't want to go, and yes, I detonated before I got home." She rubbed at her temples where an ache was forming. "I have some questions too."

Maisey breezed by and dropped off Merrick's pie and poured them both a cup of coffee. "Nice to see you two chatting. Nothing can solve a problem better than conversation and pie."

"We don't have a problem," Deanna said. Her voice was louder and stronger than she expected, but it didn't send Maisey running.

She merely lifted a brow and smiled. "Well, that's your first problem. You're lying to yourself." She spun on her shoes, which made an annoying squeak, and she walked away, grumbling something about youth and waste.

"What did she do to deserve that?" Merrick asked.

"Nothing. Okay? She did nothing, but you … you broke my heart."

His mouth dropped open like a hinge had broken and let his jaw loose. "Me? What the hell did I do to you? I planted you a garden which you still haven't thanked me for."

Her whole body vibrated from the inside out. Was it anger? Sugar?

"Fine. Thank you. I love the garden. Was it your way of saying sorry for being such an asshole?"

She slapped her hand on the table so hard his pie plate jumped several inches. "Asshole? I wasn't an asshole. You're the one breaking hearts."

"What?" she yelled.

Maisey peeked her head out the swinging kitchen doors. "Do I need to hide the knives?"

They both waved her off like they'd practiced the hand gesture together.

"I knew I shouldn't have slept with you. It was a bad idea, but things were going so well. I asked you to be sure, and you said you wanted me, but you didn't."

"Are you serious? What part of that night told you I didn't want you? It was you who didn't want me." He shoved a huge bite of pie into his mouth.

"Are you crazy? You're the one who ran away in the morning." She looked around the empty diner and was grateful that it wasn't filled with prying

172

eyes and listening ears. "I woke up to an empty bed. Imagine what that does to a girl's ego." The only people who could hear them were Maisey and Ben, who stared out the pass-through window and watched Armageddon unfold.

"You want to talk about ego?" He ran his hand through his hair. "Imagine how I felt when I'd just made love to you for the first time, and all you said was, 'At least our story is solid. No one would believe we're not the real thing now.'" He shoved his pie away. "Well, the joke is on me because I thought we were the real thing. I got up early and left you in bed because if I stayed, I would have wanted more of the fantasy, and what good would that have done either of us?"

The world slipped from under her, and she sank into a bottomless pit. "You thought we were real?"

"You're right. I'm an asshole because, for the first time in a long time, I believed there was a chance for someone to love me. You were perfect for me, but then again, we weren't real. You're one hell of an actress. Maybe you should take the stage instead of Samantha." He pulled a ten from his wallet and slapped it on the table. "Good luck with Red. At least he's transparent ... there's no hiding what an idiot he is." Merrick stood and walked away.

Deanna's whole world toppled. *What the hell just happened?* All she wanted was for someone to love her, and in her quest to find that, she couldn't see that someone did. Merrick said he made love to her. It had felt like love, but she was so caught up in everything else that she couldn't see what was truly happening. While she was trying to get Red to fall for her, she was falling for Merrick.

Stupid

Stupid

Stupid

"Everything okay?" Maisey snuck up on her, causing her to jump a few inches off the red pleather bench.

"No. It's not." The sting in her eyes turned to tears that spilled down her cheeks. "I screwed it all up."

Maisey moved into the booth beside her and wrapped her in a hug. "Oh, darlin', one mistake doesn't end a life." She pulled back. "Well, unless you take a turn off a cliff or don't pull the ripcord when you're skydiving, but generally, relationships can withstand a few of them."

Deanna threw herself back into Maisey's arms and buried her face into the collar of her shirt. Maisey smelled like maple syrup and bacon. On most days, that would lend itself to the comfort of the hug, but today it made Deanna feel lonelier.

Would there ever be a day when she and Merrick would laugh over pancakes again?

"I messed up, Maisey." She sat back and looked at the woman who raised Dalton. The same woman who mothered Samantha when she was down. Seeing the motherly compassion in Maisey's eyes made her long for her mother. "I didn't know he cared about me."

Maisey shook her head. "Most men bring you a bouquet. That boy planted you a garden."

Her chest hurt so badly. Could a person die from heartache? "Does the whole town know about that?"

The trill of Maisey's laughter filled the room. "Honey, this is Aspen Cove. Not much happens around here that people don't know about. I'm pretty sure we invented neighborhood watch. For example, Peter Larkin saw Aiden digging up some bulbs for you, so he dug up some of his overgrown irises. That got Charlie and Trig Whatley involved because they had a bunch of tulip bulbs that she never planted, so she brought them here. Ben and I grow a lot of our produce, and we had fertilizer in our shed that wasn't being used. I believe Goldie and Tilden donated a potentilla bush or two." Maisey leaned in and whispered. "Everyone knows those bushes need sun, but she planted them in the shade anyway because she likes yellow flowers.

Moving them to your place was an act of mercy for the plants."

"I had no idea so many people helped."

"Honey, you live in a community that cares, but no one would have thought to offer anything if that sexy sheriff hadn't started the project. He did that because he likes you."

"I'm such an idiot."

"Me too. I fell in love with the town drunk, but look at Ben now. He hasn't taken a drink in over a year. Love makes you do crazy stuff. Like planting a garden for someone you don't think likes you. Can't you see, he did that after he thought you'd played him. That's got to mean something."

She groaned. "Did you hear everything?"

"I may be old, but I'm not deaf. I'm pretty sure that argument could be heard into Silver Springs."

The embarrassment filled her so thoroughly, she nearly choked on it. "What am I going to do?"

"Do you love him?"

That was an interesting question. She felt things for Merrick that she hadn't felt for anyone. When she thought of him, her insides grew warm, and her heart felt full, or at least they did until that morning.

"I messed up."

"But do you think you could love him?"

Deanna nodded. "I think I could. I'm pretty

sure I already do. Oh God. I totally screwed this up. What can I do?"

Maisey tucked her hair behind her ears and pushed her glasses up the bridge of her nose. "Does he need a garden?"

CHAPTER NINETEEN

"Why would she say something like that if she didn't mean it?" Merrick was behind the sheriff's station, cleaning out the cruiser with Aiden and re-playing every word Deanna had said to him.

"Tell me exactly what she said to you that night?" Aiden sprayed the tires with Armor All and lowered to his haunches to shine them up. Too bad life wasn't as easy to clean up.

"She said, 'At least our story is solid. No one would believe we're not the real thing now.'" He raised his deep tone to a feminine pitch.

Aiden chuckled. "You have a lot to learn about women. If I were to guess, she was feeling insecure and vulnerable. She'd just done the deed and was looking for you to tell her that you were real." He did a final wipe of the tire and stood. "I can't tell you how many times Marina told me stuff just to hear me refute it. When she was pregnant with Logan, she kept telling me how fat she was."

"Why would she do that?" Merrick gathered the cleaning supplies and tucked them into the caddy.

"Because she needed validation."

"Not Marina. Why would Deanna think I didn't like her?" He leaned against the cruiser. "If she would have asked, I would have told her right then that I'd fallen for her."

"I told you to be careful." Aiden picked up the supplies and headed toward the office. "I warned you."

"I know, but how could I not fall for her. She's pretty, sweet, and makes a mean garlic chicken."

"What are you going to do now?" He tucked the car cleaning supplies into the mop closet and headed for his desk.

"I have no idea. How do I come back from something like that? I left her that morning, and I left her in the diner. I'm not that guy."

"You are now. The question is, how do you make her believe that you're the type of man who stays, and ... do you want to."

"Why wouldn't I?"

"There's still the Red issue. You need to get clarity on that before anything else."

During this whole mess, he hadn't considered that Deanna could still be pining for Red. She didn't make love to him like a woman who wanted another man.

"You're right. I need to figure it out."

The phone rang, and Aiden answered it. "Sheriff Cooper, how can I help you." He raised his hand and waved.

Merrick walked out with one thing on his mind. He needed to solve the Red issue. The only way to get to the bottom of a situation was to start where the problem began, and that was with Red.

He climbed into the driver's seat of the cruiser and headed toward the recording studio. If he couldn't find Red there, he'd show up at his door. There was no use in talking to Deanna until he knew Red's intentions.

Luck seemed on his side because he found Red taking his jack from the trunk just as he pulled onto Main Street.

With his lights flashing, Merrick pulled over. Part of him wanted to play the tough cop—the one who would swagger over and give the idiot a ticket for blocking a public driveway—but he wasn't that guy. The motto "Serve and Protect" didn't mean he only helped those he liked. It meant everyone was equal, and despite his personal feelings, he was bound to assist anyone in need.

"You got a flat?" he asked, stepping out of his cruiser and moving toward Red.

Red rolled his eyes. "You're pretty observant."

"Look, man, don't bust my balls. Do you want my help changing it or not?"

Red set the jack on the ground by the rear left tire. He stared at it like it would somehow automate and change the tire itself.

"I tried to call AAA, but they said it would be over an hour." His shoulders sagged forward. "I'm embarrassed to admit that I've never changed a tire myself."

"Seems like a good time to learn." Merrick went to the trunk and pulled the spare out. "You're lucky you have a full-size spare. These days they usually give you a mini. I've even seen the manufacturers skip that all together and only give a can of Fix-A-Flat."

Red lifted his hands into the air. "You're speaking a foreign language to me."

"It's irrelevant since you've got a spare." Merrick showed him how to set the safety triangles on the road to warn other drivers of their presence. He made sure the brake was set and took out the wrench to loosen the lug nuts before taking the jack and placing it in the correct position for stability.

"You want to pump the handle until the flat lifts off the ground. Once it's off, you can remove the lug nuts and pull off the tire."

"Why are you helping me?"

"Why wouldn't I help you?" He could probably give a dozen reasons why he didn't want to, but they wouldn't serve anyone.

"You don't like me."

"That's true, but I'll still help you."

Red stared at him for a moment and then leaned down to yank off the flat tire.

"I appreciate it."

"This turned out well for me."

Red shook his head. "It's the shits for me. Why is it good for you?"

"I was coming to see you anyway." They worked side by side, putting the new tire on. "I wanted to talk about Deanna."

"Dude, nothing is going on between Deanna and me. Apparently, there was never anything going on between you and her, either."

That little jab hurt. Merrick's inner six-year-old lashed out by picking up the flat tire and tossing it to Red, who wasn't ready. It hit him in the chest, pushing out an "ugh" sound and making him stumble backward.

"She told you that?"

"Yes, right after she told me to leave her alone."

"She did?"

"The woman hates me."

"Good, because you're not good enough for her."

Red shoved the flat back into the trunk. "You're right. I'm not good for anyone. I knew that from the get-go, but there's no convincing these women when they think they want you."

"Occupational hazard?"

"That, or a screwed-up childhood. I haven't decided what I'm going to blame this time."

"What about taking responsibility for yourself?" He knew too many people who blamed their shortcomings on their parents or used their jobs as an excuse for bad behavior. "You used Deanna."

Red chuckled. He lowered the jack and put it away along with the wrench. "So did you."

Red seemed to want to kill him by a thousand cuts.

"That's not true," Merrick said.

"Yes, it is." Red crossed his chest and stood defiantly. "The way I heard it, it was both of you who wanted something. She wanted me, and you wanted mommy off your back."

His words hit like a bullet to the heart. Maybe they were so painful because they were true. He had entered into a relationship, albeit fake, to get his mother off his back. "It may have started that way but," —he clenched and unclenched his fists—"I actually care about Deanna while you never did. She put her heart and soul into attracting you, and you tossed her away."

Red sighed. "Listen, there is a saying that goes something like this." He took a breath. "If someone shows you who they are, you should believe them. I'm an asshole."

"And you're okay with being one?" Merrick never understood that feeble excuse for bad behavior.

Red leaned against his car. "You would think you'd be happy that I am. That gives you an in." He rubbed the scruff on his chin. "I'll never be the man Deanna wants. Hell, I don't think she even knows what she wants."

I want her to want me. "You owe her an apology."

He shook his head. "I don't owe anyone anything."

"Not true. You need to say you're sorry, and you owe it to yourself to dive deep into why you think women are expendable." He pointed down the street. "I'd say it's time you talked with Doc Parker. He'll get to the heart of your problems quickly."

After kicking off the side of the car, Red moved to the driver's door. "That's the problem. I don't have a heart."

"Thanks for being an idiot." He turned around and walked away. "Just so we're clear ... stay the hell away from Deanna. She's mine, or she will be."

Merrick walked back to the cruiser. How in the hell was he supposed to win her back? Could she possibly love a man like him? In his experience, that was never the case.

CHAPTER TWENTY

Sitting under The Wishing Wall, Deanna tore the top off a cranberry orange muffin. "Have you ever thought of making cherry muffins?" She asked Katie.

"Cherry? No, would that even be good?"

"I love cherry pie, and I can't imagine anything having cherries could be bad."

"I don't know. I used to have a muffin a day, but now I've added cinnamon streusel and Sage's bran muffins, and it's totally screwing up my schedule."

"Fine," she said with a huff. "I figured if I could get one more place to get my cherry fix, I wouldn't have to hang my head. Jewel orders extra Hostess pies, and Maisey saves me a pie that I get to eat on my own. I'm surprised I haven't outgrown my jeans."

"I'm happy to try it. I opened this bakery because Bea thought I'd make a good addition to Aspen Cove. Maybe a cherry muffin will be good as an additional menu item. The thing I've learned about life is if you never take chances, you never get what you want."

"Now that I know what I want, I'm not sure if I'll ever get it. I screwed everything up."

She looked up at the corkboard and found the sticky note she'd put there. With a tug, she tore it free and crumbled it up, leaving it on the table in front of her. The only love she saw in her future was a snuggle from Sherman.

"Well, fix it."

She glanced at Katie, who was filling up the display case.

"How do you fix something when you're not even sure where you stand with someone? I mean, I thought I was in love with Red, and then I met Merrick. I thought it was all fake, but then I fell in love with him. Am I really in love or just in love with the idea of being in love?"

Katie's eyes opened wide, and a smile lifted the corners of her lips. "Well, there's no time like the present to find out."

The bell above the bakery door rang, and

Deanna turned her head toward the sound. Casting a shadow on the black-and-white tile in front of her was Merrick. His chin was set, and his jaw muscle ticked.

Deanna picked up the note and turned it over and over in her hand. She tried to avoid eye contact, but Merrick wasn't the kind of man she could ignore.

He walked to the counter. "Hey, Katie. Have you got any of those turtle brownies?"

At the mention of turtle brownies, Deanna looked at him.

The set line of his jaw softened, and a hint of a smile played at his lips. Oh, those lips ...

"I don't, but I've got some walnut fudge."

He frowned. "I was hoping for the turtle ones. A really good friend bought them here, and I've been craving them ever since."

Katie cleared her throat. "Are you sure it's the brownies you're craving?" She plated up a walnut fudge brownie and passed it across the counter to him. There was nothing subtle about Katie. The sideways nod of her head made it clear she was pushing him to sit next to Deanna. "I find that sometimes we associate food with experience. In truth, those brownies were decent but not crave-worthy. I'd say you're looking for something sweeter."

Merrick chuckled. "I'd say you're right." He attempted to pay for the brownie, but Katie shook her head. "No charge today." She wiped her hand on her apron. "I need to check on Sahara, so I'm going to turn the closed sign over, but feel free to stay inside." She hurried to the door and turned the lock, then flipped the sign to closed before she skirted off to the back room. When the rear door slammed shut, Deanna knew they were alone.

"Do you mind if I join you?" His rich voice bounced off the walls.

The bottom dropped out of her stomach, and she swore her heart slid out too and hit the worn tiles on the floor.

"Umm, no." She pointed to the chair beside her.

Here he was in front of her, and she had nothing grand to offer him.

They stared at each other for a moment. Her eyes followed him from his hair, down to his eyes, then his slightly crooked nose to those insanely perfect lips.

"I'm sorry," she said.

He cocked his head to the side. "I'm sorry too." He picked a walnut off his brownie and popped it into his mouth. While he chewed, he seemed to have a thousand thoughts rushing through his mind, or maybe he had none, and the contemplative look he had was merely him deciding on the quality of the treat he ate.

"How's work?"

"It's good. Not much changes here except poor Mrs. Brown's cat's clothes."

Deanna giggled. "Is he missing today?"

Merrick shook his head. "Not that I know of, but there's still time." He set his brownie aside, placing it on top of her note. A sense of relief washed over her. The last thing she needed him to see was how desperate she was for love. "What about you? How's work?"

She thought back to yesterday and her run-in with Red. She would have thought she'd be more upset than she was. Letting him go also released a lot of anxiety. She was still full of self-doubt, and her self-esteem was probably at an all-time low, but there was a calm that came from resignation.

"You know, it's all good until it isn't. I think we're a day or two from going on break."

"Does that mean you won't work?" He stretched out his legs.

A part of her wanted to climb into his lap and settle her cheek on his chest; to breathe in the scent she'd come to associate with him. The spicy cologne that ran through her veins like the first cup of morning coffee. Right that second, it was essential, like air or water. She leaned in and inhaled just to get her fill.

"I'll work. There are a thousand behind-the-scene jobs that need to be taken care of. I take care of all the fan stuff. I do the press releases. I pretty much coordinate everything for Samantha. In the end, I work for her. The others ..." She shrugged. "I do things for them because I'm nice that way. When we're on hiatus, I'm back to being Sam's assistant."

He nodded and then cleared his throat. "Do you really want to talk about work or ..." He paused for a moment.

"Or, I'd rather talk about ..."

He reached out and laid his hand on top of hers. The warmth from his body spread through her like molten lava. There was something there. It was a visceral connection. It didn't matter if her head wasn't so sure, her body was on board.

He swallowed hard, causing his Adam's apple to ripple in his throat. "Look, I totally messed this up." He cupped her hand and squeezed. "I should have asked about the garden, but my intentions were good. I just ..."

She moved closer. "You don't have to apologize for planting me a garden. I owe you an apology. I never knew how much my words could have hurt you. I was ... I was silly. I know better than to skate the subject. I work with men." She giggled. "No offense, but the simpler I can keep it with them, the better chance I have of them understanding."

"None taken. We are simple. Just club us over the head if we aren't picking up on your cues." His thumb rubbed over her hand. "That was what was happening, right? You were hoping I'd negate your comment about us being fake?"

There was so much hope in his voice. If she closed her eyes, she could almost see this giant mammoth of a man as a small child with pleading eyes.

"Yes, I'm so used to beating around the bush. In truth, I had hoped you would set me straight, but you didn't, so I resorted back to the game. It was easier to believe we were still playing it rather than know that you'd used me too."

"Red is right. We used each other, but not that night. That was real. Everything about us making love was us making love. I felt it, and I know you felt it too."

She laid her hand on top of his. "I did, and that's why it hurt so much that you abandoned me in the morning."

He nodded. "It was more about self-preservation than abandonment, but I can see why you would feel that way."

This was the most honest conversation she'd

ever had with a man. Being raised by a single mother didn't give her a lot of experience in dealing with men. Working with musicians didn't give her real-world experience because their lives were not stereotypical.

"Tell you what," she said. "Let's try something new. Let's build whatever this is on honesty."

"What a concept." He broke a small bite of his brownie off and held it to her lips. "I say we share everything. No secrets between us."

She took the bite and savored the rich chocolate and crunchy walnut. "I agree."

He leaned in and moved so close their lips almost touched. "You start. I need to know what your deal-breakers are."

She wanted to kiss him but knew if their lips met, they'd never get another word said, so she leaned back.

"You've left me twice, once in bed, and once at the diner. That's a deal-breaker for me. If you abandon me again, I'm not sure I'll be able to move forward. You do want to move forward, right? That's what this is all about?"

He smiled, and she swore the sun shot from his lips. He was light and warmth and happiness.

"Yes, this is about moving forward, but maybe we should start at the beginning."

"The beginning?" The middle was pretty fantastic, too, but the beginning sounded promising. "How about dinner tonight? I'll whip up some take-and-bake pizza from Dalton's. I'll even spring for a six-pack of beer."

He moved so fast, her head spun. His lips touched hers, and he spoke against them. "It's a date—a real date. This is real. Scary as hell, but real." He pressed his mouth to hers, and she melted against him. There was no coaxing needed. The minute his tongue touched her lips, she let him in. There was no dueling. No rushed pace. His kiss was soft and languid, and his tongue slipped against her like liquid gold. He tasted sweet, like chocolate and passion. There was a promise in the kiss. He was telling her he wouldn't abandon her.

Then his phone went off.

He groaned as he pulled away.

"Sorry."

He answered. "Deputy Buchanan." His forehead furrowed. "I'll be right there." He hung up.

"You have to go?"

He rose from his seat. "I do."

"See you tonight? Six?"

He brushed her lips with his. "It's a date."

She laughed. "A scary date," she teased.

He swept his brownie off the table. "Care if I take this? It might be lunch."

"All yours." She meant it. The brownie. Her lips. Her body and her heart.

He folded the wrapper over and stuck it into his shirt pocket before he turned and walked to the door. The deadbolt turned under his grip, and he walked out; only this time, Deanna didn't feel so alone.

Minutes later, Katie walked back inside. "How'd it go?"

"You didn't have to leave your shop so I could talk to Merrick." A broad smile made her cheeks ache.

"But I did, and by the looks of it, the talk was good?"

"We have a real date tonight at six. It's a do-over. Same pizza, same beer, but no fake-date bargain."

Katie boxed up a few brownies. "I don't have the caramel brownies, but I have these." She handed Deanna the box. "You can probably take your note from the wall."

"I already did." She glanced at the table, but the note was gone. "Oh, no."

"What?"

"I think Merrick had my wall wish stuck to the bottom of his brownie."

Katie threw a fist into the air. "The wall works then. It got into the hands it was supposed to."

Deanna covered her face with her hands. "How embarrassing." The best she could hope for was that he wouldn't notice and would toss it out with the wrapper.

Katie looked at the clock hanging on the wall. "Girl, you have time to doll yourself up. Hot bath. Glass of wine. Paint your nails."

"You're right. I do." She gathered her garbage and tossed it into a nearby trash can. She couldn't believe how the day unfolded. She woke up solidly in the "I'll die single" camp, and now she had a date. A real date. Maisey's words from yesterday filtered through her brain. "And I thought I'd have to plant a garden."

Katie waved her off. "All you needed was to plant a seed."

Though the sweet baker had no idea what she was referring to, her response was spot on. "Yep, the seed is planted. All I need to do is water it." As she walked out of the bakery, vines of hope sprouted inside her heart.

CHAPTER TWENTY-ONE

"What are we dealing with?" Merrick climbed into the passenger seat of the cruiser. Aiden turned on the lights and took off toward Copper Creek.

"Hostage situation. Armed robbery at a bank. The Copper Creek police department has asked neighboring communities for help. They already have two officers down."

Merrick's shoulder stiffened as a current roped through him, making the hairs stand on his arms and the nape of his neck. His shoulder throbbed where the bullet from the last hostage situation hit him.

He stared ahead but saw nothing except a replay of the events that unfolded in Denver last year.

All he could see was the fear in the little girl's

eyes as her father held the gun to her head. Silent tears ran down her face as her whole body shook.

The rage that filled him was strong enough to power an entire city. He wasn't a reckless cop, never had been, but that day, all he thought about was that man in the library who had taken his life. Any man willing to hold a gun to his child's head was a man ready to use it. He had nothing left to live for.

The hostage negotiator had failed. As far as they knew, the girl's mother was already dead. Wearing his vest, he moved toward the man but talked to the girl.

"It's Haley, right?" He held up his hands as if to surrender. Between two fingers, he held a lollipop. "Do you like grape?" He made a slow move to raise the sucker so both father and daughter could see it clearly.

"Don't come any closer," her father yelled.

"You're Todd. Hey Todd, I'm Officer Buchanan."

"If I won't talk to your negotiator, what makes you think I would talk to you?"

Merrick wasn't there to talk. He was there to take action. As one of the only cops without a family or children to come home to, it made sense that he'd be the one to enter the fray. He had less to lose, fewer people who depended on him.

"I'm not here to talk. I'm here to tell you a story."

Lying was never his strong point, and he hoped the guy didn't see the twitch in his jaw. "When I was a kid, a man held himself hostage in a library. At the time, I thought that was insane. I also thought it was noble. Two sides of the same coin. He was desperate but chose to be alone in his desperation. My mom was the librarian and managed to get everyone out of harm's way. She was the hero that day because the cops took far too long to get there." While he spoke, he inched forward, hoping his voice and the sucker he moved in his hand distracted the man.

"All I wanted was my family." Todd's voice cracked. "She ruined it all."

"Where is she?"

He looked over his shoulder, and Merrick knew it was too late for Haley's mom, but not for her. He had but a second to act. A second while Todd was distracted. A second to save Haley's life.

He bolted from his place and ripped Haley from her father's arms. He curled his body around hers and took off running. Shots rang out, with one hitting his vest with the power of a sledgehammer. Another burned a hole right through his shoulder, but he continued to run until he found cover behind the swat car.

The medical team rushed in, pulling Haley from his arms. Several more shots rang out. In seconds, a little girl was an orphan.

"Are you listening?" Aiden's voice broke through his memory.

"Yep, a hostage situation. Twenty captives, two are children. One gunman." He didn't know how he did it, but he always managed to think and hear simultaneously.

"I brought you because you have some experience with this kind of thing. Mark would be a fish out of water in this situation. The only hostage he's seen is Tom, the cat, and the poor thing escapes with regularity. Can't help a victim who returns to the scene of the crime with regularity."

"Food is a great motivator." Speaking of food, he remembered the brownie he put in his pocket and pulled it out. Stuck to the bottom of the napkin was a yellow note. He pulled it off and glanced at it.

All I want is to be seen, be heard, be appreciated, and be loved.

Deanna

Had she put it there for him to see? He had to believe this was a gift from the universe, telling him that Deanna was open to receiving his love. He took a bite of the brownie and put the note back into his pocket. When he got back to town, his first stop would be to see Deanna and tell her he was up to the task of loving her and wanting to be the recipient of her love.

He almost pulled out his phone to send her a

text, but they arrived at the scene before he could, so he tucked his thoughts about Deanna aside. Distractions were dangerous, and the situation was already risky as it was.

The Copper Creek police chief walked over to brief them.

"Shots were fired, but so far, no hostages have been injured. They seem to be warning shots, mostly aimed out the window. He clipped the first two officers on scene."

"Do we know who the guy is and what he wants?"

"He's Michael Caldwell, twenty-five, and a meth addict. The best we can tell is he's carrying a Glock, but we don't know how much ammo he's got. What he wants is for us to go away and let him leave, but we all know that's not happening. Our best bet is to get the hostages out one by one and let SWAT handle the rest."

Merrick frowned. Dealing with drug addicts at their best was tough. Put one in a powder keg and add a match with the stress of the entire Copper Creek police force breathing down your neck, and it was a disaster waiting to happen.

Another officer approached. "He wants food."

Merrick smiled. "Now you have something to bargain with."

An hour later, a dozen hostages were freed, and a Mexican food feast was delivered.

"We need to get the kids out." The chief of police rubbed at the shadow of whiskers on his chin.

"He's not giving up his trump card," Merrick said. "He's kept all the women and children. He knows people will react strongly to mothers and children in danger. We're dealing with a smart addict."

The door opened, and a small screaming child was pushed out. The little boy turned to face the door and banged on it with both fists. "Mommy."

"Get that kid out of here," Michael said. "He's giving me a headache. If you don't shut him up, I will."

Merrick tensed. His internal need to serve and protect clawed at his skin. "We need to rescue that little boy."

He moved a step forward, but Aiden grabbed his shoulder. "Looks like SWAT has it covered."

An officer from the SWAT team moved forward in full gear while the little boy pounded on the door and screamed for his mother.

"Stop," Michael yelled from a crack in the door.

"Just getting the kid," the officer responded.

"No, you're trying to trick me."

The officer held up his hands. "No, I'm just coming for the boy."

The air rang with a growl. "Shut him up. I can't stand it anymore." The shadow behind the bank window pointed the gun down. The SWAT officer bolted for the boy.

It was like watching a rerun of his event last year. A shot rang out just as the officer swept up the child. He staggered a few feet and went down hard, pinning the boy beneath him. Merrick reacted.

He took off toward his wounded comrade with Aiden trailing behind him. It took him no time to get the boy free and hand him off to Aiden. With adrenaline surging through him, he lifted the SWAT officer just as gunfire split the air. He rushed forward toward safety. As he turned the corner and rounded the building, a searing pain sliced through his leg, and he crumbled to the ground.

Everything blurred and went to black. *Oh hell, I've been shot again.* Only this time, it was worse. He felt the life drain from his body, and his final thoughts were of Deanna before darkness consumed him.

CHAPTER TWENTY-TWO

By six-thirty, she knew he wasn't coming.

"Why?" she asked Sherman, who stared up at her from his bed. "Is it too much to ask for a man to love me?" She paced the floor in front of her window. "Hell, I'd settle for a man who cared enough to show up." She stomped across the room and picked up her purse. Times like this called for pie. She hoped Maisey had a cherry one, but at this point, any pie would do. She'd even settle for a chicken pot pie.

She walked out and slammed the door. "The only thing I asked from Merrick was that he did not abandon me, and hours later, he did. I'm done."

Too keyed up to drive, she walked the few

blocks to Maisey's and took the corner booth where Merrick had left her the last time.

Louise pushed through the kitchen's swinging doors and plodded her way. "Good evening, Deanna."

She scowled at the friendly waitress. There was no reason to take her anger out on the sweet woman who probably had to work at Maisey's to feed her brood of kids. How much milk did eight children drink in a week?

"Evening, yes. Good ... nope."

She cocked her head and nodded toward the metal rack at the end of the table. "You need time to look at the menu?"

"I'll take the pie. Cherry, if you have it. Anything else if you don't."

"Okay, one piece of pie coming up."

Deanna held up a hand. "Not a piece. I need the whole pie."

Louise's eyes widened. "You sure?"

"Some days call for moderation, but this isn't one of them."

"Okay." Louise walked off.

Deanna looked around the diner. There were the regulars that came in most evenings. She knew them because she was one of them. Mostly, they were construction workers. Occasionally, she'd see the firemen. Tilden and Goldie came in at least once a week. Wes and Lydia usually ate here on Fridays after she completed her shift at the clinic.

In his corner was Doc, who sat across from Agatha. Some people had all the luck. Doc had two great loves in his life while she couldn't find one.

The pie plate plopped in front of her. Louise stood to the side with a can of whipped cream.

"Do you want a dab or should I leave the can?"

"Leave the can."

Louise set the can on the table. "Does this have anything to do with Merrick?"

It took everything in Deanna not to roll her eyes or let out an exaggerated groan. "Why should I care about Merrick?" It hurt her to say the words because she cared more than she wanted to.

"Oh," Louise's head jerked back. "I just thought." She waved a hand through the air. "I thought you two were a thing."

"Nope," Deanna said, shoveling her fork into the center of the pie. The red filling oozed from the crust. The deep crimson reminding her of the color of blood—blood that no doubt oozed from her broken heart. "We are definitely not a thing."

Louise took a seat on the bench across from her. "It's a tragedy, really."

Talking over a mouthful, Deanna replied. "You're telling me." It was a tragedy. Just when she thought the universe was looking out for her, it gave her the finger. At least Merrick did. Well, he was too much of a coward to show up and do it in person. It was a silent finger flipping her off from wherever he hid.

"Marina was just in picking up dinner for Aiden. He's at the hospital waiting for Merrick to come out of surgery."

The fork dropped from Deanna's hand. "Wait." Her thoughts froze for a second. "Merrick's in surgery?"

"I thought you knew. News travels like a speeding bullet." Her hand came to her mouth. "Probably the wrong choice of words since Merrick got shot."

"Merrick got shot?" Her heart compressed like it was caught in a vise. "Are you sure?"

"You didn't know?"

"Someone shot him in Aspen Cove?" She couldn't fathom that kind of violence happening in the charming town.

"Oh, heaven's no. He was called to Copper Creek and a hostage situation. He saved a little boy and another officer but got shot in the process."

Deanna grabbed her purse. She reached inside and took out a twenty and handed it to Louise. "Where is he?" Each word rose in pitch.

"He's at the hospital in Copper Creek. There's only one."

Deanna flew out the door and ran all the way home. She didn't bother to go into the house but climbed behind the wheel and sped off toward Merrick.

"You are so dumb," she chastised herself. "So willing to think the worst of him because he was a man." She hit the steering wheel hard enough to leave a bruise. She deserved one. If it got purple and ugly, it would serve her well to look at it and remember that every bad thing comes from bad intentions.

Merrick left her in the bakery because he got a call. That call was the hostage situation. Her irrational mind said he could have called to let her know. The sane side said he was too busy taking care of hostages and saving people to stop and text. The logical side wins.

As she followed the signs to the hospital, she mentally beat herself up. He wanted her, and she wanted him, but what if he died without knowing how much he meant to her?

The thought made her choke on a lump in her throat. Fate had been cruel before, or had it? Maybe her hook up with Red and his subsequent dismissal was fate teaching her a lesson. It was showing her what love should feel like. Red was lust mixed with need. A woman should never be so in need of affection that she was willing to accept less than she deserved.

She pulled into the nearest empty parking spot at the hospital and dashed inside the emergency room entrance. At the desk, she asked about Merrick.

"Are you family?"

"Umm, no, I'm..."

"She's his fiancée," a commanding voice said from behind her.

She spun around to find Merrick's mom standing there with two cups of steaming coffee in her hand. They were the paper cups with poker hands on them that came from a vending machine. "It looks like you could use one of these." She passed a cup to Deanna. "Follow me. I'll take you to the waiting room."

"Is he okay?"

Elsa shook her head, and Deanna's stomach twisted into knots. Was that a no or a head shake of disbelief? She wished she knew Elsa better to know.

"He's still in surgery. He got hit in a major artery and lost lots of blood."

"Oh my God." Her mind swam with scenes from her binge-watching *Life in the ER* and *Grey's Anatomy*. Loss of blood could cause secondary problems like brain damage. Then there was the injury to his leg. Would he lose a limb? "How long has he been in the OR?"

"A few hours." She led Deanna through a set of double doors and down a brightly lit hallway that smelled like antiseptic and hope. "What took you so long to get here?"

Elsa had a right to know the truth. "I didn't know he was hurt. We had a date for six tonight, and when he didn't show, I went to the diner to drown my sorrows in pie. It was Louise who told me."

"You're here now, and that's all that matters."

Was it? Her being in the hospital wouldn't help Merrick's chances. "Is there anything I can do?"

Elsa turned the corner into a small waiting room. "They are asking for blood donations. It will probably be another hour or so before we know anything."

"Okay, I'll be happy to donate."

In the room were several people she recognized. Aiden was there with Marina. Lydia was sitting next to Sage, who rubbed her rounded belly.

Would she ever know the joys of motherhood? She'd take constipation and swollen ankles just to share the creation of life with a man who loved her.

Aiden rose. "I should have called you. I'm sorry, I just didn't think about it."

She glanced at Elsa and at Beth, who now stood beside her mother. "It's not like I'm family."

"Oh, honey, you're Merrick's girl. That makes you family."

Deanna lowered her eyes. She couldn't look Elsa in the face and say what needed to be said. "We lied to you. I was never his girlfriend. We just—"

Elsa pulled her to the side. "I know." She cupped Deanna's face and smiled. "I also know there was a spark between you too. Don't you think a mother knows when her son isn't honest? Merrick didn't want me interfering."

"He loves you too much to hurt you by being honest. It was wrong, but his intentions were good. He wanted you to be happy he was with someone. He wasn't willing to give up his career and move back to Denver. Being with that woman would have required him to alter his life plans."

"Sandra showed me another side of her that day. It was like seeing a live version of Jekyll and Hyde."

Deanna thought back to that day and how her feelings were twisted with jealousy over a woman who wasn't even a threat to her fake relationship.

"Jealousy can bring out the worst in people. I know, I wasn't at my best that day either." She sighed. "I owe you an apology for being dishonest."

"Do you care for my son?"

An honest heart never lied, and hers flipped and flopped. The pace picked up, rushing blood to her face.

"I think I'm in love with your son."

Elsa smiled. "Of course, you are. Who wouldn't be? He's handsome and sweet. He protects those he loves and those who simply need protection. It doesn't hurt that he's employed. That seems to be a problem with a lot of men these days. All this split the bill, and I'll open my own door bullshit. Having a man dote on you doesn't make you less of a woman."

Beth walked up to them and stood beside Deanna. "I couldn't help overhearing." She giggled. "I heard you that night too. That didn't sound like you were faking it then."

Elsa pointed to the door. "Beth, sometimes you make me wonder. Go sit down or give your blood or get another cup of coffee. I'm talking to the future mother of my grandchildren here."

Beth laughed. "Oh my God, just wait until Merrick finds out you're planning his life again." She walked in the direction of the vending machines.

"Back to you," Elsa said. "My son looked at you like you were the sun. There was something very real there, which is why I didn't say anything. I figured you'd work it out."

"That was the plan. As I said, we had a date tonight, but he never showed up. I thought he'd abandoned me again."

Elsa pulled Deanna in for a hug. "It's not in Merrick's DNA to abandon anyone. He may step back and let his mind work out the details, but he'll never leave you wondering for long. Trust a mother's instinct. He might not have told you yet, but that boy is in love with you."

A door opened at the end of the hallway, and a doctor emerged. Elsa took a few steps forward, then backtracked to grab Deanna.

"Dr. Marsh, this is Deanna, Merrick's fiancée. Do you have news for us?"

Deanna's heart took off like a bee racing for nectar. If Merrick didn't make it, she'd end up with so many regrets.

"He's out of surgery. He had the best vascular surgeon Colorado has to offer, so I'm sure he'll heal and be back on his feet in no time."

A whoosh of air came from somewhere. When she looked around, she realized it came from her.

"Can we see him?" Elsa asked.

"Are you sure he's okay?" Deanna glanced up at the doctor, looking for anything that told her he was concerned, but she was poor at reading people. If she'd been better, maybe she would have seen what Elsa did. Could Merrick truly love her?

"He'll spend a little time in recovery, and then we'll transfer him to a room. I'll let you both know when he's ready for visitors. As for being okay, he made it out of a difficult surgery. There are risks like clotting and infection we'll be on the lookout for, but the prognosis looks good."

Once the doctor was gone, Elsa whimpered, and her strong façade fell apart. She grabbed onto Deanna and wept.

Beth came through the door and ran to them.

"Oh God, don't tell me he's dead. I'll kill him myself if he's dead." She joined her mother and cried.

"No, he's okay." Aiden walked into the hallway with Marina. The others waiting for word joined them. Before anyone else started bawling, Deanna cleared her throat. "Merrick is out of surgery and is stable. He's in recovery and should be able to see you all in a while."

Lydia and Sage walked over to Elsa. "I'm going to get my sister back home. She gets hangry when she doesn't eat hourly, and Cheetos and Sour Patch Worms aren't going to cut it. I'll check in on him later." They gave everyone hugs and left.

Aiden's eyes were clouded with concern, and the dark circles beneath them spoke to his exhaustion. "I'll stick around if you don't mind, but Poppy is watching the kids, and Marina needs to get back to them."

Elsa laid a hand on his arm. "I'm sure he'll be grateful to see you."

"Did the situation at the bank get resolved?" Deanna asked.

"It did. All the hostages are safe. The suspect didn't make it. Once he opened fire, a sniper took him out."

A shudder rushed through her. Many things could have gone differently today, but in the scheme of things, a child was safe, and Merrick was alive.

When the nurse came half an hour later and told them Merrick was awake but groggy, they all headed toward his room.

Only one person was allowed in at a time. Being the least connected person to Merrick, Deanna waited outside while Aiden, Beth, and Elsa took turns visiting him.

Elsa emerged, looking tired but happy. She held up Merrick's keys. "I'll be at my son's house for a few days until he comes home."

Deanna pulled her business card from her purse. "Call me if you need anything."

"I will." She kissed Deanna on the cheek. "My son is waiting for you." She turned to Beth. "Let's

see how fast we can get to Aspen Cove. I figure if
we got here in less than two hours, we should be
able to make it there in less than thirty minutes."

"Geez, Mom, you're not supposed to be driving
a hundred miles an hour. One day you're going to
lose your license for speeding."

Elsa laughed. "I have connections." She looked
at Deanna and winked. "Don't keep my son waiting. He needs you."

Deanna was left alone in the hallway. She
paced in front of the door for several minutes before
she got the nerve to walk inside.

Merrick lay in bed. He was so still that she was
sure he was sleeping.

"It's about time you decided to visit." He
sounded like he was choking on sand.

Deanna rushed forward and took the cup from
his tray, offering him a drink.

He shook his head. "That's not what I need."

She sat on the edge of his bed, and he winced.
"I'm so sorry. I can't seem to do anything right." She
backed away, not sure what to do.

He opened his eyes. "Come back here." He
reached for her, but his arm flopped to the bed.
"Hate being so weak."

She moved toward him. "You're the strongest
man I know. No one would ever consider you
weak."

"You make me weak."

She furrowed her brows until an ache formed between them. "How do I make you weak?" Was this where he told her she wasn't right for him?

"Weak in the knees, silly." He coughed, and his face turned unnaturally pale. "Damn, that hurts. Everything hurts." He patted the edge of the bed. "Sit with me."

"But I'll hurt you."

He shook his head. "Only if you abandon me."

Her breath caught in her throat. "Never. Haven't you heard? We're engaged." She gently took a seat on the edge of his bed, careful not to jostle him in any way.

"Yes, I heard. My mother informs me that we are having two-point-five children in the next five years."

Her shoulders shook with a suppressed laugh. She did her best to hold it in, but a squeak broke free. "What are we going to do with half a child?"

He reached out and took her hand. "I don't know. I was hoping for four in four years, but I'll settle for two."

She knew he was still full of drugs, and nothing he said should be taken seriously, but there was a part of her that hoped some seed of truth was present.

"I'm so sorry you got hurt." She cupped his face

and gently ran her thumb over the bruise on his cheek.

"I'm sorry I didn't show up for dinner."

Tears trickled down her face. "I fed your first piece of pizza to Sherman."

"I bet you were pissed at me."

What she felt then didn't matter. "Everything is okay."

"We need to talk." His eyes drifted closed, but he forced them to open again. "You need to know something."

"Whatever you have to say can wait." She wanted to bask in the glow of their fantasy life together and the possibility of having his children.

He shook his head. "No, things like this shouldn't wait. They have to be said before it's too late."

She looked into his eyes, eyes that were clouded with pain. "Tell me."

He pulled her hand, so she fell forward. Trying not to crush him, she placed her hands on either side of his head. They were mere inches from one another.

"I love you." He rose with a scowl and touched his lips to hers for a brief kiss before he sagged back against the pillow. "You need to know that I would have shown up for the date. Tonight's dinner was the first day of the rest of our lives, and I wouldn't have missed it if I could have helped it."

"I love you, too. I knew it in my heart, but my head got in the way."

He touched the skin over her left breast. "Always think with your heart, babe."

Hearing his nickname for her made her melt against him. Her lips found his, and they started a long and languid kiss.

Someone cleared their throat behind her. "Excuse me, I'll need to take his vitals," the nurse said.

Deanna gave Merrick another quick kiss and lifted from his bed. "Oh, he's alive all right. Nothing can keep my man down."

CHAPTER TWENTY-THREE

Merrick hobbled from his bedroom to the kitchen and started a pot of coffee. His mother and Beth were coming up from Denver today to stay the weekend. She'd come up every weekend since the event. He chuckled at how he described the shooting as "the event," like somehow it was planned like a concert or an outing.

"I would have put the coffee on," Deanna said. She sidled up next to him and gave him a kiss. Ever since that first day in the hospital, she hadn't left his side.

"Deanna, I don't need you to make the coffee or cook my dinner or do my laundry. Elsa Buchanan raised me, and she taught me how to be self-sufficient."

He watched her shoulders sag. "I get it. You don't need me."

He pushed off the counter to face her. The weight shift sent a jolt of pain down his leg. The doctor said that would be the case while the tissue healed, but he was certain Merrick would make a full recovery.

"Babe, I need you, but not for those things. I need you to be my friend, to love me no matter what, and to forgive me when I'm an idiot. While I like that you want to cook my dinner, clean my house, and do my laundry, those things aren't what make me love you."

The corners of her lips lifted. "Say it again."

This was a game she played, but he'd learned to play his own. "I don't need you to—"

She covered his mouth with her hand. "You know what I mean."

Yes, he did. She needed to hear the words. "How about I show you how much I love you?"

He grabbed her hand and led her toward his room. "Merrick, don't forget about what the doctor said."

He knew the doctor told him to take it easy on the leg, but Dr. Marsh didn't have Deanna lying next to him each night. It was like putting a piece of chocolate cake in front of a dieter and making them look at it each day and never take a bite. Merrick had willpower, but not when it came to his woman.

"He said all things in moderation. Celibacy is not moderation."

She rushed ahead of him, stripping off her shirt along the way. "Very true." She looked at the clock on the nightstand. "When is your mom getting here?"

He laughed. "Not for an hour."

For the next forty-five minutes, they made love, and it was love. No other woman made him feel the way Deanna did. He always thought it was his job to protect and serve, but it was okay to let someone else defend him too. Deanna was like a pit bull when it came to her loyalty and fierce devotion.

They were almost dressed when Sherman barked. He had settled into Merrick's place without any trouble. All the little guy needed was kibble, a place to run outside, and a lap to snuggle in at night.

"The watchdog has spoken. Your mom must be early." She pulled on her shirt and slipped her feet into her shoes. "I'll get the door. Are you okay to dress yourself?"

He was dreading this visit. He knew what it was about. His mother had been hinting at him to leave the force. "Once is bad luck, two is an omen," she said. He'd been waiting for Deanna to say something too. She'd been tight-lipped about "the event." Somehow avoiding it made it not real.

For the last week, they'd lived in a bubble of bliss, but today everything would change. Would he give it all up if Deanna asked him? She once said that every day a person walked out of the house could be their last, but that was before they fell in love. Love did crazy things to the heart and mind. Love could make a sane man crazy and a crazy man sane. Love was an equalizer or a disruptor. It was too soon to know which of those it would be for him.

Down the hallway, he heard his mother enter and greet Deanna. His sister's voice followed close behind.

He tugged on his shirt and slipped on his sweatpants. They were the least constricting and most comfortable of the clothes he had to wear.

Trying to hide his limp, he put on a smile that wasn't hard to fake because he'd just finished making love to the most beautiful woman in the world.

"Hey, Mom." He walked up to her and kissed her on the cheek. Turning to his sister, he knuckled the top of her head. "Hey, brat." It was funny how he still viewed Beth as his little sister when she was two years older than Deanna.

"Hey, gimp," Beth said. "Where should I put the groceries?"

"Follow me," Deanna led her to the kitchen. Sherman tagged along, hoping something would fall from the bag. He loved the visits from Beth because she always had a treat in her pocket for him.

"We stopped by the Corner Store. I swear that young woman who runs it looks familiar."

He walked to the chair by the window and took a seat. "A lot of people say that about her. I guess she has a familiar face. I can't say I've seen her anywhere but there. She's nice enough but has a weird list-making habit."

"Making lists is very efficient. I have to say that the Corner Store has a lot more to offer than I first imagined."

He shifted to get more comfortable. Though he hid the pain, his mother's knowing look told him he was fooling no one. "I told you that everything I need is right here."

"You also told me you'd be safe and look at you." Her eyes fell to his leg.

Just the weight of her stare made it ache.

"Go ahead and say it. I've been waiting for you to start in on me."

Deanna and Beth walked into the living room. "Say what?"

A taut feeling fisted his stomach. This was the argument he saw coming but wanted to avoid.

"This is where Mom tells me I should quit my job and come back to Denver."

Deanna chewed on her lip until it was plump and red. Had she been thinking about it, too, but was afraid to bring it up? So far, he hadn't met a woman who could deal with his career of choice. They tolerated it but never really embraced it, and now he prepared himself for her rejection.

Loving a cop was fine as long as he was safe, but the nature of his job meant he'd never be safe. Life was inherently dangerous, no matter the career choice. It was his job to make sure that the scales weighted toward safe for everyone, and if he left his job, no one was safer, including him.

"Merrick." His mother used the librarian tone. The "shh, you need to be quiet" voice that scared kissing teenagers out of the stacks. "I'm just asking you to be reasonable."

Deanna cleared her throat. "I agree with your mother."

His heart took a nosedive. "Come on, Deanna."

She held up her hand. "Give me a chance to explain." She took a seat next to his mother and turned to look at her. "You've raised a wonderful man. He's good and kind, and everything a woman like me could want in her forever guy."

He waited for the but.

"Except safety," his mother added.

"Yes, there's that, but ..."

There it was, the dreaded but. His natural instinct would be to fight for his job, but something held him back. Deanna had something to say, and he wanted to hear her, see her and appreciate the value she brought to his life.

"But what?" he asked.

"But being a cop is part of who you are. It's a gut instinct for us to want you to quit." She wrung her hands in her lap. "That first night in the hospital, I prayed that you would, but leaving your job doesn't make your life better, and it doesn't make you safer. It just makes us worry less, which is ridiculous. Every year tornados, earthquakes, and floods wipe out lives and homes. Those are natural disasters and aren't related to an occupation. I once read about an airline dumping the waste from a plane, and it came down in a shitsicle and killed a man watching Oprah. My point is, life is dangerous."

"You aren't asking me to leave my job?"

Mom lifted her hand. "I am. I'm not willing to see if your luck runs out."

Deanna got up from the sofa and walked to Merrick. Lowering to her hunches, she stared at him. "I'm asking you to never leave the house without saying goodbye and I love you, to live each moment with me like it's your last, and realize the only minute we ever have is the one we're in."

"How did I get so damn lucky?" He pulled her up and into his lap, sitting her on his good leg.

"You happened to be in the Corner Store, and you were a good kisser."

"Only a good kisser? I'll have to up my game."

"Well," his mother grumbled. "If I'm not getting you out of law enforcement, I better be getting a grandbaby soon."

"Mom, I haven't even asked Deanna to marry me yet."

"Oh *pish*," she said. "Get on with it. Lord knows, if your luck stays the same, there's a shitsicle heading our way right this minute."

THAT NIGHT AFTER DINNER, Beth put on her makeup and her best jeans. He knew they were her best jeans because he ponied up a hundred bucks to buy them last Christmas.

"Where are you going?"

"It's Saturday night, and I'm single. I'm going out."

His mother sat in the corner chair, reading a poetry book while he and Deanna binge-watched

Vampire Diaries. It wasn't a show he would have ever tuned into, but love made you crazy or at least altered your taste in television. As long as she was snuggled up next to him, he'd watch hours of public service announcements if it meant he could keep her there.

"There's only one place to go, and there are only three single residents that I know of. Two are off-limits, and one is too old."

"Oh my God, I'm not sixteen, I'm thirty-two, and I know what I'm doing. If I want to go to a bar, I will. If I choose to hook up with someone, I will."

Merrick put his hands over his ears and started a mantra of *la la la la*. When he saw his sister's mouth was closed, he dropped his hands. "I don't want to hear about your sex life."

"Currently, I don't have one, but that can change quickly, as you well know. Finding the one can't be that hard. All you need is the right stuff at the right time."

"Stay away from Red. He's trouble. You're too good for him."

She walked to the door and stuck her tongue out like a sixteen-year-old. "Maybe his problem is that he hasn't met the right one." Her face turned pink, and she looked at Deanna. "No offense to you."

Deanna smiled. "None taken. I owe a lot to

Red. If he hadn't been such an idiot, I might not have met your brother. Having said that, I agree with Merrick. Red is a player. He's not the kind of man who will ever settle down. If you're looking for longevity, then he's not the one for you."

Beth laughed. "At this point, I'd settle for long." She covered her mouth and laughed. "Oh, did I say that out loud?"

"Beth," Merrick warned. "I'm serious. Red isn't your forever guy."

"Fine, who are the other two?"

Deanna laughed. "There are more than two. Peter Larkin is in his eighties, but he's single. He doesn't match his socks, but I hear the ladies love him and his little blue pills."

Merrick growled. "I don't want to know." He turned to his mother. "Aren't you going to do something about her?"

His mother waved him off. "I've learned my lesson. A mother shouldn't meddle."

Deanna continued. "Gray is single but jaded. He's already got an ex-wife. There's a lawyer who lives in town whose name is Frank Arden, but he works too much. If you're looking at going cougar, there's Basil Dawson, but he's mid-twenties at best. His father is single if you have a daddy fetish."

"Hmmm." Beth put a finger to her chin. "See, brother, there's a smorgasbord of offerings."

"Do not bring anyone to my house."

Beth rolled her eyes. "As if." She blew them a kiss and walked out the door.

"She's going to be the death of me."

His mother looked up from her book. "Oh, honey, just wait until you have daughters."

CHAPTER TWENTY-FOUR

Merrick was not in bed when Deanna woke. The poor man was up most of the night worrying about his sister until he heard her walk in the front door at just after two. It warmed Deanna's heart to see how much he cared about the women in his life.

The door swung open, and he walked inside, carrying a tray with coffee and a breakfast of toast and eggs.

"You made breakfast?"

He grinned. "I did. I'm a man of many talents."

She rose and leaned against the headboard. "Oooh, breakfast in bed. You're spoiling me."

He set the tray on her lap. "I plan to keep you spoiled. You deserve good things. When I met you,

I told you that you deserved better. I'll try to be better for you all the time."

A thousand butterflies took off from her stomach and circled her heart. "I love you."

"I love you too. Who would have thought a fake girlfriend would turn into a real wife."

She cocked her head, trying to make sense of his words. It was probably him mimicking his mother's sentiments. She'd been at them all weekend to tie the knot and start the baby-making. Deanna didn't want to rush things, but her clock was ticking as well. She wanted what everyone else had. She wanted a husband, a home, a child, or two or three or four. There was no turning back the clock, but she also knew that life worked at its own pace. She'd tried to force her love on someone not open to receiving it. Now that she was with someone who loved her, she felt the difference. True love nourished the soul. It didn't suck the life and energy out of you but restored you. No, she wouldn't rush anything. There was no point in bypassing all the good stuff in the middle just to reach the end. Life was about all the things in between.

Merrick sat on the edge of the bed and handed her the juice. "Drink it up." He smiled. Not his usual sweet smile, but the smile of a six-year-old up to something.

If Merrick wanted her to drink her juice, she

would. She took a sip and set it down. His eyes went to the cup several times.

"You know what else I'm good at?" He lifted his brow in that seductive way he did that made her heart beat faster and her panties melt.

"Oh, I know how good you are at that."

He puffed out his chest. "Well, I am, but that's not what I'm talking about."

She raised her glass and took another sip of juice. He sat up tall as she drank and sagged when she placed the cup back on the tray.

"Tell me."

"Turns out, I'm an excellent internet shopper. I'm also quite skilled at research. Did you know there are four Cs when it comes to diamonds?" He picked up her glass and handed it to her.

"Carat
Color
Clarity
Cut"

Her entire body tingled, and heat rose to her face. There was only one reason a man would talk diamonds with his girlfriend, and it wasn't because Sherman was getting a studded collar.

She gulped down her juice, and on the last drink, something hit her lip. When she pulled the glass away, she looked inside the cup to find a ring with a single solitaire sitting on a white gold band.

"What are you asking me?" She knew what this meant, but she had to hear the words.

He tried to slide to the floor but winced when he was halfway down.

He pulled the ring from her glass and put it in his mouth. She watched him move it around, and when he pulled it back out, she stared at a stunning princess cut that was now shiny and clean.

"In a perfect world, I'd be on one knee. You wouldn't be in bed, but in a beautiful dress at Trevi's Steakhouse or on the beach with a waterfall as the backdrop, but this isn't a perfect world." He shifted his body, so he faced her, and he took her left hand into his. "I bought this ring before I ever left the hospital. I knew the perfect opportunity would present itself. Yesterday you said we only have the moment we're in. Deanna Archer, I don't want to spend another minute without knowing you're mine. If you'll take me, I'd love to spend the rest of my forevers with you." He held the ring to her fourth finger and waited.

"Merrick Buchanan, I always thought there were four things I needed as a woman. I needed to be seen, heard, appreciated, and loved. I know that I have made my fair share of mistakes, but I have learned that you have to make mistakes to know when you find the right thing, and you, Merrick, are it for me. So, yes, I'll give you all my moments, and we can spend those moments together, creating our perfectly imperfect world."

He slipped the ring on her finger and kissed her like there was no tomorrow because there was no guarantee.

THEY EMERGED from the room fifteen minutes later, acting like giddy school kids. Elsa and Beth sat at the kitchen table, drinking coffee.

Deanna held out her hand. "He asked me to marry him."

Both women oohed and aahed at the ring. "Where did you get it?"

Deanna laughed. "Apparently, he's a good internet shopper."

Beth rolled her eyes. "You bought her ring on Amazon?"

Merrick took Deanna's hand and stared at the diamond. "No, I bought it from James Allen. It's not a conflict diamond, and it's nearly flawless."

Deanna giggled. "It would be the only flawless thing about me."

He cupped her face and pressed his lips against hers. "You're perfect for me."

Elsa clapped her hands. "Oh, good. I was

starting to feel guilty about poking holes in all of your condoms."

"You what?" Panic rose in Beth's tone.

"Well, it was obvious they were meant to be together, so I thought I'd help things along. Then I felt guilty for meddling."

"Mom." Merrick narrowed his eyes. "You said you were going to stop meddling."

"Oh, I have. I poked the holes last weekend while I was here. This weekend, I've been a saint."

"Oh, shit," Beth groaned and buried her face in her hands.

OTHER BOOKS BY KELLY COLLINS

Recipes for Love

A Tablespoon of Temptation

A Pinch of Passion

A Dash of Desire

A Cup of Compassion

A Dollop of Delight

A Layer of Love

Recipe for Love Collection 1-3

The Second Chance Series

Set Free

Set Aside

Set in Stone

Set Up

Set on You

The Second Chance Series Box Set

A Pure Decadence Series

Yours to Have

Yours to Conquer

Yours to Protect

A Pure Decadence Collection

Wilde Love Series

Betting On Him

Betting On Her

Betting On Us

A Wilde Love Collection

The Boys of Fury Series

Redeeming Ryker

Saving Silas

Delivering Decker

The Boys of Fury Boxset

Making the Grade Series

The Dean's List

Honor Roll

The Learning Curve

Making the Grade Box Set

Stand Alone Billionaire Novels

Dream Maker

GET A FREE BOOK.

Go to www.authorkellycollins.com

ABOUT THE AUTHOR

International bestselling author of more than thirty novels, Kelly Collins writes with the intention of keeping love alive. Always a romantic, she blends real-life events with her vivid imagination to create characters and stories that lovers of contemporary romance, new adult, and romantic suspense will return to again and again.

Kelly lives in Colorado at the base of the Rocky Mountains with her husband of twenty-seven years, their two dogs, and a bird that hates her. She has three amazing children, whom she loves to pieces.

For More Information
www.authorkellycollins.com
kelly@authorkellycollins.com

Made in the USA
Monee, IL
05 August 2023

40495911R00138